L.A. JONES

RISE OF THE SHADOWMARES

ORCHARD BOOKS

338 Euston Road, London NW1 3BH

Orchard Books Australia

Level 17/207 Kent Street, Sydney, NSW 2000

First published in the UK in 2012 by Orchard Books

ISBN 978 1 40831 471 5

Text © L. A. Jones 2012

A CIP catalogue record for this book is available from the British Library.

1 3 5 7 9 10 8 6 4 2

Printed in Great Britain

Orchard Books is a division of Hachette Children's Books, an Hachette UK company

For Andrew Smalley, my other half

L.A. JONES

RISE OF THE
SHADOWMARES

ORCHARD

PROLOGUE

Quentin Bane stood transfixed.

He knew that he was dreaming because everything was slightly hazy. The tall figure with a black cloak and top hat hovered in front of him, his thin grey hair cascading down his shoulders. His nose was shaped like a hook. His eyes were as black as coal and as narrow as the slits on a moneybox.

'Are you ready?' Vesuvius asked in a scratchy voice. He crept towards Quentin, raising his cane which had a human skull on top.

Quentin felt a shiver run down his spine. He peered around his grimy cell. Graffiti covered the walls and damp and mould poisoned the air. *What am I doing?* he wondered. *I'm a rebel. A hardened criminal. I've never taken orders from anyone. Why am I taking them now?*

'I hope you're not having second thoughts?' Vesuvius hissed, as if reading his mind. He raised his skull cane again, and Quentin flinched.

'No, Master. I am at your command.'

Vesuvius's lips curled into a smile. 'Good,' he said,

lowering the cane. 'I have visited you in your dreams every night for the past six months. You were all alone, Quentin, and I was there for you. Me. The only one.'

'I know, Master. I owe you my life.'

'Indeed you do. Is everything still in place for tomorrow?'

Quentin nodded, hands trembling by his sides.

'You had better not disappoint me.'

'I won't let you down. You can count on me, Master,' Quentin said, with a hint of desperation. He wanted to please Vesuvius, more than he'd ever wanted to please anyone before, but he had no idea *why*. It was a burning desire deep in his soul, which had grown stronger every night, like some sort of disease. Sometimes he wondered if he was going insane. But he couldn't ignore it any longer. The voice, the dreams, what they were telling him to do...

Quentin's eyes snapped open.

He climbed out of bed and slid his hand underneath the mattress. He glanced through the bars into the dimly lit corridor.

No guards. Good.

He pulled out a knife and a small rock and begun sharpening the blade. He smiled. It was almost time. Tomorrow the bloodshed could begin.

1

Andrew, his twin sister Poppy and their mum sat staring at the TV, robotically shoving forkfuls of spaghetti bolognese into their mouths. *Happy Families* was on, the worst show *ever*.

Andrew cleared his throat. 'Pass me the pepper, will you?'

'*Shh!*' Poppy hissed. 'Doug's about to reveal he's having an affair!'

'Oh, wow, highlight of my day,' Andrew muttered, rolling his eyes. As he reached over the table and grabbed the pepper pot, a searing pain cut through his head.

'*Hurry up. I'm waiting,*' a chilling voice rasped. It sounded as if it was coming from inside his mind. Was he going crazy?

Andrew stiffened, dropping the pepper pot. Its contents spilled all over the table.

'Did you hear that?' he asked, looking around.

'Hear what?' his mum said, not taking her eyes off the TV.

It was so loud… Why hadn't she heard it?

'A voice,' Andrew said. 'It sounded like…' He knew what he wanted to say. *It sounded like Vesuvius.* Andrew's stomach filled with dread as images of Vesuvius and his army of Shadowmares, with skull-like bodies draped in darkness, filled his head. What if Vesuvius stole Andrew and Poppy from their dreams again? What if he took them back to Nusquam, the parallel universe where the Nightmare Factory existed? A shiver ran down his spine.

No. That was impossible. Vesuvius, Master of the Nightmare Factory, was dead. Andrew had defeated him.

Hadn't he?

'Like who?' Poppy asked. She turned away from the TV. Her eyes were locked on Andrew's, full of concern. 'Who did it sound like, Andrew?'

'I don't know,' he lied. He didn't want to worry her. 'It was nothing. Probably just my imagination.' He ran a sweaty hand through his hair, shivering again as he remembered the terrifying Fear Pods, deep underground in the Nightmare Factory. They were machines which extracted children's fear in order to make Nightmares, and Andrew and Poppy had been strapped into them whilst the Shadowmares searched through their minds for their deepest fears.

He couldn't go back to that dreadful place again. He *wouldn't*.

'Are you OK, dear?' Mum asked. 'You look pale.'

Andrew nodded. He picked up his fork. His mouth felt as dry as sawdust, and the spaghetti stuck in his throat as he tried to swallow it. What if Vesuvius had found a way back, just like Andrew had dreamt he would almost three months ago?

Andrew pushed his plate away. 'I'm not hungry,' he said, getting up from the table. 'I'm going to bed.'

He hurried upstairs to his bedroom and went to the chest of drawers. He pulled out a bundle of clothes until he found the dreamcatcher hidden underneath them. He held it up, tracing his finger over the willow hoop, which was decorated with beads and feathers.

A lady called Tiffany Grey, who had helped Andrew defeat Vesuvius in the final battle, had given it to him as a gift. It was supposed to protect him from Vesuvius, so that he couldn't steal Andrew from his dreams again.

Andrew walked over to the window, searching for a place to hang it. He had a feeling that he was going to need it.

'What are you doing?' Poppy said, making him

jump. He turned around to find his twin sister standing in his doorway.

'It's just in case,' Andrew said, tying the dreamcatcher to the curtain rail. 'Maybe you should do the same with yours.'

'Why?' Poppy said, grabbing him by the arm and staring deep into his eyes. 'You think he's coming back, don't you? Why did you run away from the dinner table like that? What did you hear?'

Andrew sighed, and sat down on his bed.

'I heard Vesuvius. I think it was him, anyway. He sounded so angry.'

'Well, what did he say?'

'He said, "Hurry up, I'm waiting." What do you think he meant by that?'

Poppy sat down next to Andrew, squeezing his shoulder gently.

'I think it was all in your mind. You defeated Vesuvius. He's gone. You locked his spirit in a soul-catcher. Oran hid it—'

'I know, I know, somewhere it could never be found. But what if somebody's discovered it and let him out? What if Vesuvius has found a new body to live in and—'

'Listen, bro,' Poppy said, putting an arm around

him. 'I realise this is hard for you. It's hard for me too. But what happened three months ago is in the past. You've got to learn to put it behind you.'

Andrew nodded. But that was the problem – he *had* put it behind him…until today. Until he'd heard the voice…then all the fear and worry had crept back. Didn't Poppy understand that it was different for Andrew? He was the Releaser. His fear was more powerful than anyone else's, which meant if Vesuvius got hold of it again, he could use it to cross over to Earth. He could make nightmares that were real, and he would bring chaos upon the whole world. Andrew shuddered. It didn't even bear thinking about.

'Well, I'm going to leave the dreamcatcher up anyway…just in case,' he said, lying back and pulling the covers over him. He wouldn't let Vesuvius capture him. Not again.

Poppy shrugged, rising to her feet. 'Whatever makes you happy, bro, but honestly, you've got nothing to worry about. Trust me.'

'I hope you're right,' Andrew muttered when she'd left the room, 'I really hope you're right…'

The next morning, a knock at the door rattled all the way through the house.

'I'll get it,' Andrew said, running down the stairs with his toothbrush between his teeth. He opened the door. Dan, Andrew's best friend who he'd met at the Nightmare Factory, was leaning against the porch, grinning widely from ear to ear.

'What are you so happy about?' Andrew said through a mouthful of toothpaste.

Dan stepped inside. 'It's my first day at Fairoaks, man.'

Andrew walked into the kitchen and spat into the sink. 'Oh yeah, I forgot. Better get ready for the head-flush!' he grinned, ruffling Dan's hair.

'Huh? Head-flush?'

'Yeah, didn't you hear? All the new Fairoaks kids get their heads flushed down the toilet. It's sort of an initiation thing.'

Dan's eyes widened.

'He's joking,' Poppy laughed, running down the stairs. 'Don't listen to him.' She slung her school bag over one shoulder.

'Oh,' Dan said, folding his arms. 'Yeah. Course, I knew that.'

'Hadn't we better get going?' Andrew said, glancing at his watch. 'We'll be late if we don't hurry.'

They stepped outside into the early morning light.

The first autumn frost coated the ground in a thin layer of crystals. Andrew tugged open the garage door and they grabbed their bikes from inside. They cycled down the street, cutting into a muddy lane barely sheltered by skeletal trees. In the distance, the grey school building rose into view.

'Last one there buys snacks at break time,' Andrew yelled, whizzing down the hill. He turned to see how far the others were behind him. A splitting pain cut through his head, as if his brain was being ripped in two.

'*Ow!*' he yelled. His mind whirled. The trees and the pavement merged together, melting into a blurry watercolour of shapes and patterns. Seconds later, he was spinning headfirst over the handlebars and hurtling straight for a brick wall.

When his vision came back into focus, he was in a room surrounded by metal bars and dusty brick walls. A stale smell lingered in the air. *Where the hell am I?* Andrew thought. His heart was pounding against his ribcage with the force of a drum. *Am I in hospital? Oh God.* A wave of fear flooded through him. *I'm back in the Nightmare Factory.*

But wait. There was a man dressed in blue, lingering outside the bars. He was wearing some sort of guard's uniform, with a ring of keys attached to his belt.

Andrew read the man's badge. It said 'Belmarsh Prison'.

So I'm in a prison. But why? The last thing he remembered was falling off his bike.

He took a step forward. The walls were covered in drawings of skulls and crossbones and hundreds of nametags.

Never pick up a dead man's gun, someone had written with a black marker pen. *Three days until freedom*, another had carved into the brickwork. Andrew's eyes flitted to the next piece of writing.

Free Vesuvius. Free Vesuvius. Free Vesuvius. Free Vesuvius. Over and over, the name was scrawled with terrifying clarity. For a second, he couldn't breathe. His heart was frozen inside his chest. Surely it was just a coincidence.

But what if it wasn't?

A rasping voice filled the room, making Andrew jump.

'Wake up, Quentin. It is time.'

Andrew spun around. *Vesuvius.* He was sure of it. There was no mistaking that deep and foreboding tone. He glanced around the room, scanning the empty shadows. But nobody else was there.

A loud cough echoed against the stone walls. A stocky man ripped back the blanket and sat up in bed. At first Andrew thought it was Vesuvius, but when the man turned towards him, he could see his greasy black hair, draped like wet seaweed over his muscular shoulders. He was wearing a bright orange jumpsuit, with the sleeves rolled up to show off his faded tattoos.

'Use the knife, Quentin. Kill him,' the voice boomed. It was inside the room. Inside Andrew's head, louder than his own thoughts.

Impossible.

Yet the prisoner, Quentin, cocked his head as if he'd heard the voice too. His eyes were fixed firmly on the wall like he was in a trance, as if he was…*sleepwalking.*

Quentin moved his hand down towards his pocket. Tiny beads of sweat trickled down his forehead. Slowly, he pulled out a knife.

Andrew took a running jump and threw himself onto Quentin's back, grabbing his hair to try and hold him back.

'*Don't do it!*' he screamed. The prisoner yelled and thrashed about and Andrew tumbled to the floor, rolling several times before he came to a stop.

'Who's there? Show yourself!' Quentin yelled. Andrew gasped. Quentin couldn't see him.

'It is the boy I told you about,' the voice hissed. 'But do not worry, forget about him. We must carry out our plan.'

The prisoner nodded, and wedged a large hairy hand through the bars.

The guard marched up to Quentin, hands on hips. 'What's going on?' he asked.

Quentin smirked, grabbed the guard by his collar, and stabbed him. The guard collapsed to the ground.

Icy laughter filled the air. Andrew opened his eyes. He was back in the school lane. Poppy and Dan were staring down at him. His bike was beside him, warped and bent, with brambles tangled in the wheels.

He looked down at his hand. He was grasping a tuft of black, greasy hair. *Quentin's hair.*

Which meant only one thing: it had all been real. Vesuvius was alive.

2

'Andrew! Are you alright? You're been out cold for two whole minutes,' Poppy said, leaning over him. She wiped tears from her eyes. 'I thought you were really hurt.'

'I'm fine,' Andrew said, trying to sit up. Pain gnawed through his body. He pulled his cycle helmet off. His mind was spinning. His arms were wet with blood and he had a huge rip in his trousers. He lay back down, head pounding, lips dry.

'Water,' he croaked.

Poppy took out a sports bottle from her bag and handed it to him.

'Thanks,' he said, and gulped from it thirstily.

'What happened?' Dan asked. 'Why'd you crash?'

'I don't know,' Andrew said, the dizziness subsiding. 'I couldn't see where I was going, and I got this massive headache.' He bit down hard on his lip, wondering whether or not he should tell them the rest. 'Something really strange happened. I went... somewhere else.'

Poppy and Dan looked at each other, then back at Andrew.

'What do you mean you went somewhere else?' Poppy said. 'You were right here with us the whole time. We were watching you.'

'No. In my head.' The moment he'd said it, he wished he hadn't. He sounded like an insane person. But he couldn't keep it to himself.

He breathed a long sigh, and told them everything.

Poppy slumped down beside him. 'Oh, I see,' she said, giving Dan a look. 'So, you think Vesuvius is behind all of this?' Her voice was thick with doubt.

'You hit your head pretty hard when you fell,' Dan said. 'It was probably down to that.'

Frustration flooded through Andrew. *Why didn't they believe him?*

'No, something's happening. Something *bad*. I heard Vesuvius last night and now today, in this weird vision. It's got to mean something. Maybe I had a premonition. We should go to the prison and warn them.'

'And say what, man? They'd think you were crazy,' Dan said.

Was he crazy? He didn't know any more. He'd been

under a lot of stress recently from everything that had happened. He let out a deep sigh. 'You're right,' he said. 'I should just try and forget about it.' He glanced at his watch. The glass face was completely shattered. The hands had frozen on a quarter to nine. 'Great, and now my watch is broken.' He sighed again. 'Come on, we'd better get going. I have no idea what time it is, but I'm pretty sure we're late.'

'Wait,' Poppy said, grabbing Andrew's arm as he moved to stand up. 'You can't go into school looking like that.'

Andrew peered down at his arms and legs, which were covered in scratches. He brushed a hand through his straw-like hair, which was matted with drying blood.

'Can you heal yourself?' Dan asked. 'You still have your abilities don't you?'

Andrew nodded. Ever since Vesuvius had captured him, Andrew had experienced strange powers. Oran had explained that Vesuvius had been so fixated on finding him, that some of Vesuvius's powers had leaked into Andrew. At first, things had only happened when he was really angry or sad, but then Tiffany Grey had taught Andrew how to control his abilities and he'd discovered that he could move things with his mind,

21

shoot light out of his hands and heal himself.

'I don't think that's a good idea,' Poppy said. 'Tiffany and Oran warned you not to do things in public. Someone could see.'

'There's no one around. He'll be fine,' Dan said. 'Besides, you said yourself he can't go into school looking like that.'

Poppy mumbled something under her breath, but then nodded, stepping out of the way.

Andrew shut his eyes, and concentrated hard. He hadn't used his powers in months. Would he still remember how? He tried to focus all of his energy on healing himself. A bright blue light glowed like an aura around his entire body. Soon every vein was buzzing and pulsating under his skin. He opened his eyes. A rush of bliss washed over him as one by one, each cut faded away, like water evaporating under a hot sun, and was replaced with new pink skin.

A shocked gasp echoed out from behind them.

They spun around, spotting a face between the trees. A boy. He had curly brown hair and dark, staring eyes, and he was wearing a black hoodie. The boy blinked, snapping back to life, and then turned, sprinting through the trees.

'Hey,' Dan called after him. 'Wait.' But there was no reply.

Andrew felt his stomach twist into knots. The boy had seen *everything*.

3

'What did I tell you?' Poppy said, throwing her hands in the air. 'I warned you someone might see.'

'He appeared out of nowhere,' Andrew said. 'How was I supposed to know that he was there?'

'Who was it?' Dan stepped forward and peered into the trees with Andrew.

'I dunno, but whoever he was, I think I scared him away.'

'Maybe he didn't see anything,' Dan said. 'Maybe he just turned up at the very end.'

'Yeah, sure,' Poppy snorted. 'And Bob's your uncle. What if he tells someone? How would we explain ourselves then?'

Dan waved a dismissive hand. 'Oh, come on, even if he did, nobody would ever believe him. Besides, we'll probably never see him again anyway.'

Poppy nodded. 'I suppose you're right.'

'I am?' Dan said, frowning. 'I mean, good. Of course I am.' He got back on his bike. 'Can we go now? I really don't want to be late on my first day.' He turned to Andrew. 'Want a ride, mate?'

Andrew looked down at his own bike, a twisted heap of metal, fit only for the scrap yard.

'Yeah, alright,' he said, stepping onto the stunt pegs and holding Dan's shoulders. 'Thanks.'

They cycled through the large iron gates. 'This is way bigger than my old school,' Dan said, pedalling faster.

The school building was a huge grey block of concrete with windows. It was ugly and looked out of place in the green playing fields that surrounded it.

They dropped their bikes off at the rusty bike sheds, and pushed open the double doors. They passed through the maze of corridors, filled with bright posters of students' work from the previous term – most of which were covered in graffiti.

Andrew stopped outside their classroom, easing open the door as quietly as possible. They sneaked inside, tiptoeing towards the back.

'Miss Lake, Mr Lake, you're late. Are you looking for a detention?' a nasal voice said.

Andrew rolled his eyes and turned slowly around.

Their teacher, Mr Sharpe, was studying them

through half-moon spectacles, holding the register tightly against his chest. He was dressed in a brown crinkled suit and bow tie.

'No, sir,' Andrew said. 'We've got the new boy with us. He was lost. We showed him the way here.'

'So what happened? Did you get lost too?' Mr Sharpe asked in a patronising tone. He sighed, and his face softened slightly. 'Oh, very well. You're excused, but don't be late again.' He turned to Dan. 'And you must be Daniel Bage, I presume?'

'Yep, nice to meet you, sir.' Dan said, grabbing his hand and shaking it energetically. Mr Sharpe coughed loudly, snatching his hand back as if it had been contaminated with germs.

'Right, well, err, now seems like as good a time as any to introduce our two new students to the class.'

Andrew paused. *Hang on. What was that? Two new students?*

He knew Dan was one of them, but who was the other? His eyes darted around the room, searching the familiar faces until his gaze fell over a boy with dark curly hair. *The boy from the lane.* A cold chill ran through his body. The boy's black hoodie was draped over his chair, and he was wearing a freshly ironed Fairoaks uniform.

'Jason, would you like to come up to the front, please?' Mr Sharpe asked.

Jason stood up and began walking over to them, his cheeks flushing redder with every step.

'Class, I'd like you to welcome Daniel Bage and Jason Crab to the class.'

Everyone began clapping. Andrew nudged Poppy in the ribs. 'That's the boy!' he whispered. 'The one hiding behind the bush.'

'Are you sure?' she asked, continuing to clap.

'Positive,' Andrew said. 'So much for never seeing him again.'

'Don't use your powers in public, that's what Tiffany—'

'Yeah, yeah.' Dan groaned. 'You were right. We were wrong. So what do we do now?'

'Nothing,' she said through gritted teeth. 'We're just going to have to wait and see if he says anything.'

They shuffled over to the empty table behind Jason's.

'Just act cool,' Poppy whispered.

Mr Sharpe began taking the register. Out of the corner of Andrew's eye, he could see Jason glancing back at him every few seconds. *Please don't talk to me,* he thought. *I'm a terrible liar.*

'Right, everybody pair up,' Mr Sharp said. 'I have a quiz for you. Let's see if you still remember what you learned last term.'

'Hey,' Jason whispered.

Andrew felt his heart sink. He looked up.

'Can I be your partner?'

Andrew looked at Poppy and Dan, eyes filled with horror.

'Go ahead,' Poppy whispered.

Andrew turned back around, forcing a smile. 'Sure,' he said. 'Why not.'

Jason grinned, and shot up from his seat, hurrying over to him. He pulled up a chair next to Andrew's.

'So, erm…what brings you to Fairoaks?'

'My aunt. She's lived in America for most of her life but now she's back,' Jason said. 'My parents wanted to buy a bigger house so that she could come and live with us.'

'Cool,' Andrew said. He fiddled nervously with his blazer collar. Jason was staring at him in awe like he was some sort of celebrity. It was unnerving.

'I saw you fall off your bike earlier. Are you OK?'

So he really had seen everything. There were no maybes about it.

Andrew shrugged, trying not to look bothered.

'Yeah, it was pretty bad. But I'm alright. So, umm, you going to the Halloween dance tomorrow?'

'Maybe. If I can find a costume in time,' Jason said. He leaned in closer, eyes sparkling. 'By the way, what you did this morning – I think it was *amazing*.'

Great. So we're back to that. 'What do you mean?' Andrew asked, his voice cracking.

Jason smiled. 'You know…healing yourself.'

Dan scoffed from beside Andrew. 'Look, man, you must be seeing things. He's not Superman.'

'Don't worry, I'm not going to tell anyone,' Jason said, pulling out his phone from his pocket. 'It was just so cool. I've never seen anything like it before. Look, I caught it all on camera. I've been playing it back to myself, wondering how you did it, but—'

'You did what?' Poppy shrieked, rising from her chair.

'Don't worry, I won't show it to anyone,' Jason said, clutching the phone against his chest. 'The last thing I want to do is cause any trouble. Far from it. I think it's amazing, what you did. At first I thought it was some sort of magic trick, but it's not, is it? You have some sort of power.'

Andrew stared at the video on the phone. The blue light was radiating from his body like he was a human plasma ball. His mind whirled with panic, imagining the clip being spread all over the internet.

'You have to delete that,' he said.

Jason smiled. 'So you admit I'm not crazy then? You really do have powers?'

'Yes, fine. He admits it,' Dan said. 'But dude, you gotta delete that video before someone sees it.'

'Alright,' Jason said. 'No problem.' He began pressing buttons on his phone. 'There, it's gone now. Happy?'

Andrew grabbed the phone, flicking through the video clips. He sighed with relief. 'Yes. Thank you.'

'No mobile phones allowed in class, Andrew,' Mr Sharpe said, raising his voice. 'You know that. Put it away or I'll have to confiscate it.'

'Sorry, sir,' Andrew said, turning to Jason and handing back the phone. 'Look, thanks for deleting it, but what were you doing spying on us anyway?'

'I wasn't spying. I was looking for conkers.'

'Conkers?' Dan said, frowning.

'Yes. I collect them. See?' He reached into his pocket and pulled out a shoelace full of shiny brown horse chestnuts. 'Listen, I deleted the video clip when you asked. The least you could do is explain what's going on. I deserve to know the truth.'

'Will you give us a second?' Andrew said, pulling the others to one side.

Jason shrugged. 'Sure.' He put his head down, concentrating on the worksheet.

Andrew dragged Poppy and Dan to one corner of the classroom.

'What do you think?' he asked. 'I mean, he seems like a pretty nice kid. And it's not like he's threatening to tell anyone.'

'How do we know that we can trust him though?' Poppy said. 'He could be fooling us.'

'I think we can,' Dan said, biting his lip. 'I mean, he just wants to know what's going on, man. I think I would too if I'd seen what he had. And he deleted that video clip when we asked him to. Besides, he's new and he hasn't got any friends. Maybe we should just cut him some slack.'

'You're right,' Poppy said. 'Again.'

Dan grinned. 'Yeah, I usually am.'

'OK, that's decided then,' Andrew said.

They sat back down.

'Alright, we'll tell you. Meet us at lunch time in the common room and we'll explain everything.'

As soon as lunch time came, they made their way

down the corridor to the common room. It was an old classroom, which had been turned into a chill-out area for students. There was a TV and a foosball table, along with two tatty sofas and a vending machine. When they arrived, Jason was already there, sitting on a sofa watching TV. He switched it off as soon as he saw them.

'You alright, guys?' he said, glancing up.

'Yeah. How'd you get here so fast?' Andrew asked.

'I had Geography next door.' Jason grinned. 'So, you gonna tell me how you got your powers then?'

'*Shh!*' Poppy hissed, glancing over at the two year tens playing chess in the corner. Dan and her sat down on the sofa opposite Jason.

Andrew paced nervously up and down the room. He'd never told anyone about the Nightmare Factory, and now he was about to open up to a complete stranger. How would Jason react? Would he even believe him? Panic rose in Andrew's throat like bile, as a terrifying thought crept into his head. What if Jason blabbed to the whole school?

4

It felt so…*weird*, like he was giving a piece of his soul away. But along with fear, there was a part of him that also felt excited. The three of them had been carrying this burden around for what seemed like forever, and now, finally, the idea of sharing it with someone filled Andrew with relief.

'Listen, Jason, you're probably not going to believe a word I say, but it's the truth. Everything I'm about to tell you really happened.'

'Try me.' Jason said with a grin.

Andrew took a deep breath, and came and sat on the arm of the sofa. 'Well, it all began with a terrible nightmare. A man named Vesuvius was chasing me through a dark alleyway. And then all these skeletal creatures floated up out of the shadows, trying to reach out to me, to grab me.'

Jason brushed his hand through the air in dismissal. 'Everyone gets nightmares,' he said. 'I have them all the time. What's that got to do with being able to heal yourself?'

'Just listen,' Andrew said, leaning in closer. 'The next day, Poppy and I went into town. Some bully started harassing her. He stole her money. I went over to stop him, but he started pushing me around. Then something really weird happened. I pushed him back, and he flew across the road like a truck had hit him. I'd never possessed strength like that before, but I just put it down to adrenaline.'

Jason nodded. 'That makes sense. I've heard stories where people have been so fuelled by fear, they've moved burning cars off their loved ones and stuff.'

'Yeah, well, anyway,' Andrew said, keen not to get off topic. 'A woman named Tiffany Grey saw it all. She'd been at the market that day looking for me. She gave us some dreamcatchers and said they'd protect us from our nightmares. To tell you the truth we were pretty freaked out and decided to throw them away.' He let out a sarcastic laugh. '*Big* mistake. That night we both woke up in the Nightmare Factory after having the very same dream. The Shadowmares had stolen us from our sleep and taken us there.'

Jason sat upright, perching on the edge of the sofa. 'What's the Nightmare Factory?'

'Exactly what it says on the tin, mate. They make nightmares for the whole world,' Dan said. 'The

Shadowmares read the kids' minds and shape shift into their greatest phobias. And then the fear's used to make nightmares for everyone on Earth. But Andrew's fear is different. He's what they call a "Releaser", someone whose fear is so powerful that it can be used to make nightmares that come alive. It also gives the Shadowmares and Vesuvius the ability to cross over into our world.'

The two tenth years, who had been sitting playing chess, put the board away and strolled out of the room, leaving the four of them alone.

'And then what?' Jason asked.

'Luckily, Oran helped us escape,' Poppy said. 'It's a very long story, but he owns the Dream Factory next door. It makes good dreams instead of bad.'

'Strange things started happening to me,' Andrew said. 'I could heal myself, and move things with my mind. Oran told me that Vesuvius had been spending so much time and energy concentrating on finding me that he'd accidentally transferred some of his powers into me. We travelled back to Earth, and Tiffany trained me to control them. When Vesuvius started releasing my fear, we defeated him. We locked his spirit in a soul-catcher so that he'll never be able to harm anyone again.'

Jason frowned, and ran his fingers through his curls. 'I don't know. I think you're making fun of me. This whole thing, it sounds like something out of a horror movie.'

Andrew smiled. 'Don't I know it? But seriously, we're telling you the truth.'

Jason shot up from the sofa. 'I'm thirsty,' he said. 'I think I need a drink.' He walked over to the vending machine and began slotting his money inside. The machine groaned and a can of Coke moved slowly towards the edge of the glass. Then it stopped.

'Great, it's jammed,' he said, rattling the machine.

'Don't,' Andrew said, getting up. 'I'll do it.'

Jason frowned, moving aside. Andrew held his hands up against the glass, focusing all of his energy on the Coke can.

'OK.' Jason grinned. 'But I don't see how that's going to…' His voice petered out.

There was a burst of purple light, and the can rattled like it was about to explode. It shot free and dropped into the drawer below. Jason bent down and picked it up.

'How'd you do that?' he whispered.

Andrew shrugged. 'I told you, Vesuvius transferred some of his powers to me.'

'You really were telling the truth…' Jason said, his eyes widening. 'What else can you do? Show me more.'

'Not now,' Andrew said. 'Not in school. Come on, let's go and get some lunch.'

The four of them headed back down the corridor and towards the cafeteria. The stuffy hall was packed full of children, and muddy footprints covered the floor. A loud bustle of voices carried through the room, along with the screech of metal chairs. Some kids were sitting with lunches brought from home, others had school dinners.

'What's for lunch?' Dan asked, taking off his coat and hanging it on a chair.

'Burger and fries on a Monday,' Andrew said. 'Quick, let's get in the queue before they run out.'

They hurried and joined the long queue of children.

Dan's face turned grey.

'What's wrong?' Jason asked. 'Don't you like beefburgers?'

'Mate, is that who I think it is?' Dan said, ignoring him. He pointed a shaky finger at the woman behind the counter. She was wearing a white pinafore and was busy dishing up burgers and fries.

'Who?' Jason asked.

'A new dinner lady, so what?' Andrew said, turning back around.

Dan shook his head. 'No, man, take a closer look.'

Andrew sighed, and stood on his tiptoes to look again at the woman. His eyes locked on her hooked nose and dark beady eyes and his stomach tightened with dread. '*Madam Bray?*' he gasped, so loudly that it made several children in front of him turn around and stare.

'What's wrong? Who is it?' Jason asked.

'Unbelievable,' Poppy said. 'Who does she think she is, coming *here*?'

'*Who?*' Jason said for the third time. For a minute Andrew had forgotten that he was even there.

'Madam Bray,' he said. 'She was stolen from her dreams as a child just like us. But she formed an alliance with Vesuvius and ended up working for him at the Nightmare Factory, as a dinner lady.'

Jason stopped dead, the colour draining from his face. 'She's from the Nightmare Factory?'

Dan nodded. 'Uh-huh. Pure evil.'

'Right,' Jason said nervously. 'And she's, like, on Vesuvius's side still?'

'Yeah, man, she's crazy. The last time we saw her she tried killing Poppy with a bladed Frisbee.'

Jason frowned. 'I wonder what she's doing here.'

Andrew snorted. 'Exactly'. Madam Bray's sudden arrival was too strange to be a coincidence.

The queue moved forward, and they soon reached the counter. They were standing face to face with Madam Bray for the first time since the final battle with Vesuvius twelve weeks ago. Andrew stood staring at her, unable to tear his eyes away. Her hair was short and spiky and her usually taut cheeks had gained some weight. Her gaze darkened slightly when she saw them, but then she looked down at the counter, slapping a burger and fries onto each of their trays.

'That was weird,' Andrew muttered, as they hurried across the hall and found a table at the back of the room. 'She completely ignored us.'

'I know,' Poppy said, pulling out a chair and sitting down. 'Do you think she even recognised us?'

Dan snorted loudly. 'Of course she did. She was ignoring us on purpose. The only thing I don't get is why she would want to come and work here. She hates children. Especially us'

'Didn't you say she was a dinner lady at the Nightmare Factory though?' Jason said.

Dan stared at him. 'Yeah, so?'

'Well then, it's her job. Maybe she's just doing what she knows best.'

Dan let out a sarcastic laugh. 'I don't think so, man. There's more to it than that. It's like, why *here*? *Why at this school?*'

'You're right,' Jason said, sucking from a carton of orange juice. 'Stupid idea.'

Poppy chewed on a nail. 'It doesn't make any sense. It's like she's come here to spy on us or something.'

The words sent a shiver down Andrew's spine. He began to feel dizzy. The room was spinning, faces merging into one another.

'Something's not right.'

'Not right?' Dan said, shoving a handful of fries into his mouth. 'Dude, that's the understatement of the decade.'

Andrew wasn't listening. He clung to the edge of the table, feeling a horrible sickness crawling into his throat. 'Not again,' he whispered, as the piercing voice screamed inside his head, filling his insides with a terrible coldness.

Find it! Kill whoever you must! Do not let anything stand in your way.

Images of a man running through a busy street flashed through Andrew's mind. At first he didn't recognise who it was. He was wearing guard's clothes and carrying a gun. He reached two policemen, and Andrew saw the flash of coldness in his dark eyes.

The convict from his vision. Quentin Bane.

His finger slid slowly over the trigger.

'Kill them!' the voice urged, and Quentin aimed the gun directly at the policemen.

'No!' Andrew shrieked.

There was the crack of a gunshot. It was so deafening, it pierced Andrew's ears like a dagger. Quentin Bane fled down the street until he came to a majestic building supported by six stone columns. He stopped, and moved towards the revolving door, clutching the gun by his side.

Andrew opened his eyes.

Dan put a hand on his shoulder and he jumped backwards. The bright fluorescent lighting in the cafeteria stunned him back to his senses.

'Are you OK?' Poppy asked, frowning at him from across the table.

Andrew blinked. His head was throbbing like his skull was being pushed apart 'What just happened?'

'Mate, you tell me,' Dan said. 'One second you were eating your fries and the next you were screaming about a man with a gun.'

Andrew peered around the cafeteria. Children were chatting, some had their chairs slung back, feet resting on tables. Some of them were eating. No one had seen what he had seen. He looked down at his sticky palms. He was drenched in sweat, his shirt clinging to his skin like glue.

'I don't know.'

He jumped up from his seat and stumbled outside into the cool breeze. He crouched down against the cafeteria wall, putting his head in his hands.

The others had followed him. 'Maybe you bumped your head harder than we thought when you fell off your bike?' Poppy said, putting a soothing hand to his forehead. 'You've got a temperature. I think we should go and see the nurse.'

'No.' Andrew said, gasping for breath. His voice sounded like his throat had been rubbed down with sandpaper. 'Listen to me. It's got nothing to do with the bike crash. I had another vision. These things that I've been seeing... I think they're really going to happen.'

Jason frowned. '*Visions*? What do you mean?'

'I keep on having these weird out-of-body experiences. It's as if I'm watching someone else's life, like I'm a fly on the wall. There's this convict who

I saw escape from prison and I heard Vesuvius's voice telling him what to do. I saw him running through a street, killing two policemen.'

A long silence hung in the air.

Jason licked his lips, looking pale. 'Erm, Andrew, I think there's something you need to see.'

Andrew stiffened. 'What is it?'

'Come to the common room and I'll show you.' He turned and walked quickly away, and Andrew, Poppy and Dan had no choice but to follow. They hurried along the brightly lit corridor until they reached the common room. Once inside, Jason ran over to the sofa. There was an older boy and girl sitting on it snogging. Jason grabbed the remote control from beside them.

'I saw this earlier, but I didn't think anything of it until now.'

'What?' Andrew said again, but Jason ignored him. Instead, he pointed the remote at the TV and changed the channel. The news flashed up onscreen.

The boy and girl on the sofa stopped kissing.

'Hey man! What are you playing at?' said the boy, jumping up. 'We were watching that.' He puffed his chest out, trying to look tough.

Jason spun around. 'No you weren't. You were too busy cleaning out her tonsils.'

The older kid's eyes narrowed and his face darkened in rage. 'Change it back now or I'll make you.'

Andrew didn't want a fight. 'Come on, Jason, let's go,' he said, but Jason wasn't backing down.

'Oh yeah, I'd like to see you try.'

The boy looked down at Jason, hesitating, as if deciding what to do next. His fists were clenched by his sides. 'Come on, Nick,' the girl said, grabbing his hand. 'Let these idiots watch their stupid news programme. We've got better things to be doing.' She giggled and kissed him on the cheek again. This seemed to soften the boy's anger because he turned and they fled the room together.

'So, tell me, what did you need to show us that was so important that you almost got yourself killed?' Poppy said, hands on hips.

Jason laughed. 'I didn't almost get myself killed. I could have handled him.' He coughed. 'Anyway,' he said, nodding towards the screen. 'Look.'

'Breaking news! The murderer Quentin Bane has escaped from Belmarsh Prison...' read the caption at the bottom of the screen.

Andrew's heart hammered faster and faster against his chest. He could feel the sweat trickling down his forehead.

'The convict...' he whispered, unable to believe what he was seeing.

'What?' Poppy said, her face paling.

Jason turned up the volume.

'A manhunt is under way in central London after Quentin Bane, who is currently serving two life sentences for the murder of three people, and attempted bank robbery, escaped from prison at 8.45 this morning. The thirty-three year old convict killed two prison guards, with a further four said to be seriously injured. Police are warning the public not to approach Bane under any circumstances and that they are working with the military to try and detain him.'

Wait, 8.45? Andrew froze, the words repeating around his head. But that was the exact time his watch had stopped. The same time he'd crashed his bike. Which meant only one thing. Andrew swallowed, feeling his throat grow tight with dread. It wasn't visions of the future at all, but glimpses into the present.

He knew where Quentin Bane was, and it was up to Andrew to stop him.

5

'W eird,' Poppy said, switching off the TV. 'I wonder why you're having visions about him.' She frowned. 'I think we should call Tiffany and Oran. If this has anything to do with Vesuvius, they need to know.'

'You're right,' Andrew said, getting his mobile phone out. 'They'll know what to do.'

'Oran?' Jason said. 'The guy who owns the Dream Factory?'

'Yes.' Poppy nodded. 'We can trust him. Oran saved us from the Nightmare Factory and helped us defeat Vesuvius.'

Andrew began frantically dialling Tiffany's number.

A calm voice answered on the other end.

'Tiffany?' Andrew panted. 'Have you heard about Quentin Bane yet?'

'The escaped convict? Yes, why?'

'I think Vesuvius helped him escape. I don't know why, but I saw it in a vision.' He explained about the hallucinations he'd been having as quickly as he could. 'Look, I know where he is. The last time I saw him, he was outside the Bank of England. We need to warn the police.'

Silence.

'Hello? Tiffany, are you still there? We've got to call the police and tell them we know where he is. He might kill more people.'

'No police,' Tiffany said quickly. 'Andrew, meet me in town as soon as you can and bring the others. I'll let Oran know right away.' With that, the line went dead.

'I don't get it,' Andrew said, slipping the phone back in his pocket. 'She doesn't want us to call the police.'

'Why not?' Dan said.

'I don't know. She told us to meet her in town. Maybe she wants to check it out first and see if it really has got anything to do with Vesuvius.'

'OK,' Poppy said, nodding. 'We'll go and see her as soon as school's over.'

'No, she said to come now. We'll have to ditch school.'

'Is she crazy?' Dan said 'It's my first day. I'll get expelled.'

'I don't think she would have asked without good reason,' Andrew said.

Dan nodded. 'You're right, man. How much money has everyone got? We'll grab a taxi.' He reached into his trouser pocket and dumped a handful of coins onto the table. 'I've got two quid.'

'Three,' Poppy said, doing the same.

'I've got five pounds,' Jason said, placing a crumpled note on the pile.

The others stared at him.

'Jason, you don't have to do this. We don't expect you to,' Andrew said. 'You can walk away now and nobody would think any less of you.'

'Yeah, I know, but it sounds like you could do with my help.' He grinned. 'Plus I've got History next anyway. I *hate* History.'

Andrew smiled. 'Come on then,' he said, running towards the door.

They hurried across the playground. The nerves rose up in Andrew's stomach like an ocean swell. He'd never bunked off school before, but what they were involved in was so much more important than a few detentions.

They reached the large iron gates. Several of the dinner ladies were crowded around nearby, deep in conversation.

'What now?' Jason said, crouching behind the wall.

'We sneak straight past them,' Andrew said. 'One by one. Hopefully they won't notice us, but if they do, *run*.'

'And you think that's going to work?' Poppy said, raising an eyebrow. 'They'll call the *head teacher*, and then we'll really be for it.'

'Well have you got any better ideas, clever clogs?'

She shrugged. 'No.'

They stood up, peering through the iron gates.

'Come on, let's just go,' Jason said, walking out. Poppy and Dan looked at each other, and then followed, both tiptoeing by unnoticed. Andrew set off. He passed through the gates and walked down the hill.

A warm sensation drifted through him. He'd got away with it. No one had noticed.

Then a voice. Screechy, familiar. 'Where do you think you're off to?'

Andrew froze. He turned slowly, and saw Madam Bray tapping her foot on the pavement. He scowled at her.

'None of your business.'

Madam Bray's mouth folded into a menacing smile. 'I wouldn't wander the streets alone if I were you. Haven't you heard that Quentin Bane has escaped from prison?' She leaned in closer, and her breath smelt as if something had died in her mouth. 'It's very dangerous out there, especially for little boys like you.'

Andrew pulled back. 'I'm not a *little boy*. I can look after myself, you know. And anyway I don't know what you're doing here. Since when did you care about my safety?'

Wait. What was he doing? Every second that he stood here, letting her wind him up, was an extra second he could be stopping Quentin Bane, and working out what the hell all this had to do with Vesuvius.

He broke into a run, not looking behind him until he reached the others.

'We have to get a move on – Madam Bray saw me leave,' Andrew panted, tugging off his tie and blazer and shoving them in his school bag.

He stepped onto the kerb and raised his hand, hailing the first black cab that he saw. It pulled over, and they tumbled inside.

'Skipping school?' the balding taxi driver asked. He tutted loudly.

'That's none of your business,' Poppy said through gritted teeth. 'Just drive us to the Bank of England, please.'

'Can't. The whole area's been closed off because of Quentin Bane.'

'Great,' Dan said. 'The whole area? Are you sure?'

'I've just driven straight past it. They've got a four-mile radius swarming with police. It's dangerous with that madman lurking around the place. You should be in school where it's safe.'

'Yeah, yeah, we know,' Andrew said. 'Just take us as far as you can then.'

'Fair enough, it's your choice,' he said, pulling away. Andrew twisted around to look out the rear window. Madam Bray was hobbling down the street, furiously shaking her fists at them. Andrew waved sarcastically back at her.

He turned back around, tension running through his veins. 'She knows something that we don't.'

'You're right about that,' Dan said. 'But what?'

'I'm sure we'll find out soon,' Jason said, eyes straight ahead.

They rode through the busy streets of London, passing joggers and cyclists and weaving their way in and out of traffic. Eventually the taxi stopped next to a large metal barrier. The street, usually full of busy office workers and shoppers, was teeming with patrol cars and police dogs. Tape with the words 'Police, Do Not Cross' was wrapped around a lamp post and reached all the way across to the other side of the street. Hordes of journalists had gathered, shouting at the police officers for information.

'This is as far as I can take you,' said the taxi driver.

'Cheers,' Andrew said, getting out of the car and handing him the fare.

They pushed through the crowd of journalists to the barrier.

'What now? We're never going to be able to get past,' Dan said, looking at the stern-faced officers with shields and submachine guns who were guarding the barrier. 'I don't know what Tiffany was thinking.'

'Ye hath little faith,' said a familiar voice from behind them. Andrew turned to see Tiffany's grinning face. Her green eyes were as bright as a cat's. Her long black-and-grey hair stood out against her fair skin like coal on snow.

'Hey, Tiffany,' Andrew said, giving her a hug. 'Where's Oran?'

'I'm here,' said a deep voice. Andrew scanned the crowd, and spotted a tall man with a purple top hat stumbling towards them. His white hair tumbled over his shoulders like a wizard's. Andrew had forgotten how tall he was. He towered over everyone, drawing even more attention to himself by wearing a lime-green suit and carrying a unicorn horn.

'It's so good to see you,' Andrew said, throwing his arms around Oran's waist.

Jason cleared his throat.

'Oh yeah, this is Jason. He's new at our school. We've told him everything and he wants to help.'

Tiffany cast a wary glance at Jason. Then she smiled. 'Hi, Jason,' she said. 'Listen, we don't have much time. We need to get to the bank as soon as possible. Quentin Bane is a bank robber.'

'So?' Dan said. 'What has that got to do with us?'

'That's what I thought at first,' Tiffany said. 'Until I found out about Andrew's visions. Vesuvius has been penetrating Quentin's dreams, helping him escape.'

'But…what does Vesuvius want with him?' Poppy asked.

'Oran hid the soul-catcher in one of the high-security vaults in the Bank of England,' Tiffany said. 'So I think you can guess what he wants with him. We really don't have time to stand around chatting. We need to get there before he does.'

Dan gasped, and Andrew took a step backwards. He didn't want to believe it. He bent over, his stomach churning. If Quentin Bane found the soul-catcher, that was it. Vesuvius would take over Quentin's body and he'd be free again.

Andrew put a hand to his mouth. 'I think I'm going to be sick.'

'Me too,' Poppy said, turning pale.

'No time for that now,' Oran said. 'Be sick in your own time. We've got to get moving. I've found a route around the back that is only being guarded by a few police officers. I think it's going to be the easiest way inside.'

'One problem,' Dan said. 'How do we get past them?'

Oran held up his pearly unicorn horn, which shone as if it was made from moonstone. 'I'll send them into a trance using this.'

Of course… It had got them out of trouble so many times before.

'What is that thing?' Jason asked.

'You'll see,' Andrew said, grinning. 'It's pretty cool.'

"We may need your powers too,' Oran said, looking at Andrew. "So be prepared to use them if you have to."

Andrew nodded.

They crossed the street and sneaked into a narrow alleyway where they came up against two armed police officers.

'There's no access beyond this point, sir. Please go back the way you came,' said the taller of the two men.

Oran carried on moving towards them. Andrew and the others followed closely behind.

'Excuse me, sir. Did you hear me?' the officer said, tightening his grip on the gun. 'I told you to turn around and go back the way you came.'

'Sorry,' Oran said. 'But we can't do that.' He held his unicorn horn up in the air and the alleyway was filled with a blast of bright light. Andrew shielded his eyes from the iridescent glow radiating from the long spiral horn.

The police officers dropped their guns, staring into the horn as if it was some kind of hypnotic pendulum. Andrew slipped past them, followed by Poppy, Dan and Jason. They sprinted down the eerily quiet alleyway. The slow gushing of a fountain in a nearby square seemed like the only sound for miles. They stopped outside the bank

Andrew heard footsteps behind him. He spun around.

Another police officer. 'Freeze! Hands in the air,' he shouted, pointing a gun at them.

Andrew took a deep breath, gathering all his energy, and slowly raised his hands. When they were halfway up, he projected a shard of light out of each palm.

The light hit the officer's gun, sending it flying across the floor. Andrew wiped the sweat from his forehead, relieved that it had worked. The officer stood frozen, staring at his gun, which was now just a lump of melted steel.

'Get out of here,' Andrew told him.

The police officer nodded quickly and bolted in the other direction. He didn't even bother to pick up his hat which had slipped off his head.

'Whooa!' Jason breathed. 'That was wicked!'

'Thanks,' Andrew said, unperturbed. 'Quick! Through here.' He pushed open the revolving door to the bank. Andrew, Jason, Poppy and Dan hurried inside. Andrew gasped. The place was huge, with great white pillars holding up a majestic ceiling. They scrambled towards the lift, their footsteps echoing against the marble floor.

Tiffany and Oran appeared through the door.

'In here,' Dan called to them, beckoning them over.

They ran for the lift and clambered inside.

'Which floor is the vault on?' Andrew asked.

'Bottom.'

He pressed the last button on the lift and it descended quickly, making Andrew's belly feel as if it was turning inside out. Suddenly, the lift ground to a halt, throwing Andrew off his feet. The lights flickered above them, sending dancing shadows over the walls. Then they were plunged into darkness. Everything fell deathly silent.

Andrew heard Poppy's shaky voice from beside him. 'What's happening?'

'I'm not sure,' Oran said, hitting all of the buttons on the lift to try to get it working again. 'I think someone's cut the power.'

'Who would have done that? Nobody even knew we were coming here,' Jason said.

'Somebody did.' Andrew took a long sigh. 'Madam Bray saw us leaving. She must have guessed.'

A pain shot through his head, like someone was slicing it in half. He slid down the wall, groaning in agony.

'Andrew?' he heard Tiffany say. 'Are you alright?'

'No. I'm starting to feel dizzy again. I think I'm about to have another vision.'

There was a flash of light as Oran held his glowing unicorn horn up in the air. The pain in Andrew's head sharpened. He saw Poppy's blurred face move towards him. 'Andrew?' she was saying. 'Are you OK?' But seconds later everything turned black.

For a while, Andrew just lay there. But as consciousness started to seep back in like the first rays of dawn, he sat up, suddenly aware that he wasn't in the lift any more.

No. He was somewhere else. Somewhere he'd never been before. But where? There was a black marble floor and four solid steel walls, lined with boxes with keyholes on them.

I'm in the vault, thought Andrew.

Heavy footsteps echoed towards him, and the room lit up with an eerie blue light.

Quentin Bane appeared through the doorway. His eyes were glossy and vacant. It was like looking through windows into nothing but space. Andrew wondered if there was anything behind those eyes at all. Was Quentin aware of what he was doing, or was he simply a robot, with Vesuvius controlling the gear stick inside his brain?

Quentin moved stiffly towards Andrew, in a trance. Andrew froze, feeling his mouth turn dry.

Wait. Bane can't see me, Andrew reminded himself, relaxing a little.

He watched as the prisoner pulled out a small silver key, covered in blood. Andrew shivered as a few drops splashed to the ground. Still wet, still fresh. Who had he killed to get it? A police officer? A security guard? Andrew swallowed, trying not to think about it.

Bane moved slowly towards the security box, inserting the bloody key.

'Yes, that's it, open it!' A cold voice spilled out into the room.

Andrew jumped.

Vesuvius. His voice seemed louder than ever now, as if it was coming from inside the room, echoing, bouncing against the metal walls.

He's inside the locker, Andrew thought.

'No!'

Bane spun around, cheek twitching, eyes searching the room in panic. He had sensed Andrew's presence somehow. 'Who's there?' he said.

'*The boy is here,*' Vesuvius hissed. '*He is watching us, but do not worry. He cannot interfere. Quick! Release me. Do it now!*'

'No!' Andrew screamed again, rushing forwards to grab hold of Bane, but his hands seemed to slip through him as if he was made of smoke.

He watched Quentin Bane carefully lift the soul-catcher out of the vault. The glass jar with Vesuvius's skull inside was bigger than Andrew remembered.

'*Do it. Do it now,*' the skull hissed, black eyes burning red.

Quentin nodded and began to tug at the stopper.

6

Andrew's eyes snapped open. He was back in the lift. The others were crowded around him.

'What did you see?' Tiffany asked, crouching over him.

Andrew jumped to his feet.

'He's already done it. Quentin's found the soul-catcher.'

'What?' Dan said. 'So we're done for? It's over?'

Andrew shook his head. 'No. Not yet. We need to get down there and stop him from setting Vesuvius free. Oran, you need to make this lift work. *Now.*'

'I'll try,' Oran said, and he raised his unicorn horn in the air, filling the lift with a warm glow. Poppy and Jason screamed as the lift jerked and shot downwards. Andrew grabbed the handrail, stomach dropping. His heart jumped into his throat as they plummeted to the ground. The lift came to a sudden halt, throwing them onto their backs.

'Come on, we need to hurry,' Andrew said, getting up from the floor and prising open the doors with his fingers. 'Which way to the vaults?'

'Follow me,' Oran said, taking them down a long white corridor. They came to a metal door. There was a man slumped against it, head bowed.

'Is…is he dead?' Jason asked.

'Probably,' Andrew said, his throat closing up as he spoke. 'There was blood on Quentin's hands when I saw him in my vision.'

Tiffany bent forwards, tilting back the man's head to check his pulse. She coughed awkwardly, standing back up. 'I'm afraid he hasn't made it.'

'Vesuvius made Quentin murder him to get the key. He won't get away with this,' Andrew said, anger racing through his body. He pushed open the vault door, flying inside.

Quentin Bane was standing in the centre of the room. He had removed the stopper from the soul-catcher and thick black smoke was rising slowly out of the skull's eyes, filling the vault with a poisonous smell. Andrew put his hands to his mouth, choking on the fumes. The smoke spiralled upwards, twisting around the room like a snake. It explored every crack and crevice as if it was alive, until it finally began circling around Quentin Bane, faster and faster like a tornado, engulfing him.

Andrew lunged forwards. 'Quentin, don't let him get inside you. He wants your body. He'll *kill* you.'

The prisoner's eyes looked even more crazed than usual. A thin smile slipped over his lips. He opened up his mouth and let the black smoke slip inside.

Andrew felt a storm of dread rush through him. Quentin's blue eyes were turning completely black. His long hair changed from dark to cobweb white, and his rosy face became pale and gaunt. Quentin's lips parted again, and when he spoke, it was Vesuvius's guttural voice that drifted out.

Andrew lifted his hands up and aimed them at Vesuvius. A blast of light shot out, but Vesuvius stepped aside as fast as a bullet, and the light fired into the steel wall behind him.

'It's too late, Andrew,' he said, turning to look at him directly. His smile widened into a sickening grin and a deep, chilling laugh filled the air. Bright purple light shot out from Vesuvius's body. Andrew squinted, shielding his eyes from the glow, and when he looked again, Vesuvius was gone.

7

'Where'd he go?' Jason asked, pacing around the room. 'How could he just disappear like that?'

'He's gone back to the Nightmare Factory,' Oran said. 'He can't stay in this world without the Releaser's fear.'

'You mean Andrew's fear?' Jason said slowly.

'Yes.' Oran nodded.

Andrew looked ahead, eyes blazing defiantly. 'He's not going to get it. Not again. Not this time.'

'I hope you're right,' Oran said. 'But you'll need to start using your dreamcatchers from now on. Vesuvius will be trying to steal Andrew back. And that could mean going through all of us to do it.'

Jason gulped. 'But I don't own a dreamcatcher.'

'I've got one at my house that you can have,' Tiffany said. A siren blared from somewhere in the distance. 'Quick, let's get out of here before we get arrested.'

They ran up six flights of stairs to the main part of the

bank and out into the cold winter air.

'Where now?' Andrew shouted over the sound of spinning propellers. He glanced up to see a police helicopter flying overhead.

'Back the way we came,' Oran said. His grey hair was being whipped in every direction. He lifted his unicorn horn up ready. 'There's just enough power left in this thing to daze whoever we run into.'

'What do you mean?' Jason said.

'It's like a battery. It has a certain amount of power in it, and once it's used up, it has to recharge itself again.'

'Oh,' Jason said, looking disappointed.

They hurried past several office blocks, ducking behind a park bench as two soldiers marched past. They reached the barrier that was being guarded by at least ten policemen, armed with plastic shields and metal batons. One of them turned around.

'*Oi!* How'd you get in here?' he said.

Oran's unicorn horn began to glow brighter, and the policemen's eyes misted over like steam on a mirror.

'Let us through,' Oran said.

The policemen nodded, swaying from side to side, as they parted to let them past.

'Well, that was easy,' Jason said when they had reached the crowd of journalists again. 'Man, I'd love to have some sort of power. It would be amazing.'

'It's not as good as it looks,' Andrew said.

'Yeah,' Dan said. 'With great power comes great responsibility.'

Jason laughed. 'Isn't that from Spider-Man?'

Dan shrugged. 'Probably, but it's true!'

Tiffany stuck her hand out and a black cab pulled over to the kerb.

'Camden, please,' she said to the driver.

The driver nodded, and they drove off down the road.

'So what now?' Poppy whispered.

'Now?' Oran said, breathing a long, heavy sigh. 'Now we concentrate on keeping Andrew safe. There's nothing more we can do.'

'I need to know why I keep having all these visions.' Andrew said. 'Why could I hear Vesuvius? Why could I see what he was doing?' He felt dirty and unclean, like he wanted to scrub all those horrible memories from his head.

'We think it might have something to do with the connection forged between the two of you,' Tiffany said. 'When Vesuvius's emotions are heightened, if he's angry or scared or excited about something, you get a snapshot into his mind. That's why you can hear his thoughts.'

'Huh?' Poppy and Andrew said at exactly the same time.

'Think of it like this,' Oran said. 'Imagine two radio stations. They each exist on their own frequency, but sometimes, due to storms or other interference, the frequencies become entwined, the wires become crossed and you can hear both transmissions at the same time. I suppose it's a bit like that.'

'So can he see into my mind?' Andrew asked, afraid of thinking anything at all.

'I'm not sure,' Oran said. 'But you said Vesuvius always knows when you're there, watching. I think you'd feel him if he was in your head, like he can feel you.'

'But how did Vesuvius make Quentin Bane break into the bank?' Jason asked. 'He doesn't have a connection with him.'

'No, but he had control over his dreams,' Andrew said, realising he'd known this deep down all along. 'I expect he has been visiting him in his sleep these past few months, speaking to him more and more each night, gaining his trust.'

'That's right.' Oran nodded. 'Vesuvius needed someone who was lonely and didn't have much contact with other people. Someone whose mind was already weak. A mind he could penetrate easily. And, of course, he also needed someone who had the skills to break into a bank. That's why he chose Quentin. He was the ideal puppet.'

Poppy nodded. 'That makes sense.'

Jason sat staring out of the window, unusually quiet. Andrew wondered if he regretted getting involved. He didn't blame him if he did.

The cab pulled up outside Tiffany's house and they hurried inside. It was full of even more unusual plants than Andrew remembered, colourful vines twisting around the banister and up the walls as if part of the paper.

'Your house looks like a jungle,' Jason said, looking around. 'The plants…they're such weird colours.'

'I'm a herbologist.' Tiffany smiled, placing a plate of cookies on the table. 'In other words, I grow plants to make into herbal potions to help people. There's nothing that can't be cured with the right flower or tree. Most of the plants here are from Nusquam, my native land. That's why they're such *weird* colours, as you put it.'

'I wouldn't get too close,' Andrew warned him, just as a red plant with large blue leaves began to wrap itself around Jason's arm.

'*Arghh!*' Jason screamed, yanking backwards. The leaves tightened their grip, and the veins on his arm bulged to the surface of his skin. 'Get this thing off me!'

Dan collapsed onto the sofa, laughing.

'Stop that,' Tiffany said to the plant, as if it was a pet dog. She pulled a knife from her pocket and threatened the plant so that it recoiled back into its pot. 'Some of them are a bit mischievous at times. You just have to show them who's boss.'

'Right,' Jason said, backing away and standing in the doorway instead.

Poppy took a cookie off the plate, holding it in her hands instead of eating it. She was still sitting on the sofa, but had her legs curled up into a ball. 'Vesuvius can't harm us, right?' she said, frowning. 'I mean, he needs Andrew's fear to make nightmares become real again. And the Shadowmares can't cross over without it.'

'That's right,' Oran said, bending his head as he came through the doorway. 'As long as you sleep with your dreamcatchers, you should be safe. He can't harm you.'

'Well, that's a relief,' Jason said, still clutching the dreamcatcher.

'But what about the prophecy?' Andrew said, sucking in air. 'We didn't defeat Vesuvius the first time. He came back. So surely that means one of the futures will still come true?'

'What prophecy?' Jason said, glancing up.

Andrew looked at Tiffany. 'Can I tell him?'

She faltered, and then nodded. 'I suppose so, he knows everything else. I don't see what harm it could do.'

Andrew turned back to Jason, shuffling on the sofa as he did so.

'A few years ago, Tiffany had a dream. Nusquarium people can't physically dream, so on the rare occasion that one of them does, it's considered an omen.'

Jason came and sat on the arm of the sofa. 'So what happened in it?'

Andrew took a deep breath, feeling his chest tighten. 'In the dream, she saw two possible futures. The first, I died, the world was completely destroyed and Vesuvius ruled over everything. In the second, the world was returned to normal and I lived. Tiffany wrote it all down in a book which so far, Vesuvius knows nothing about.'

Tiffany hurried out of the room. When she

returned, she was a carrying a big leather book, which was worn at the spine.

'It's all written down in here,' she said, handing it to Jason.

He flicked through the pages, eyes bright with interest. 'My God...so Vesuvius doesn't know anything about this?'

Tiffany shook her head, and smiled. 'Not a thing. And hopefully, that's the way it's going to stay.' She plucked the book from his fingers. 'I'm going to put this somewhere safe.'

'But all of this is irrelevant anyway, right?' Poppy said. 'Because Vesuvius doesn't have Andrew's fear, and he can't cross over to get it.'

Andrew got up and began circling the living room.

'Exactly. It's too easy... Vesuvius has got to be planning something. He's *always* planning something. He's had a taste of my fear now, and he won't ever be content until he gets more.'

There was a long silence as Dan, Poppy and Jason peered around the room to see if either Tiffany or Oran had anything to say about this.

Oran let out a heavy sigh. 'Unfortunately, I fear you may be right.'

'He is?' Dan said, with a panicked expression. 'So what do we do?'

'I think you should enter his mind again, Andrew. You have a type of portal into Vesuvius's brain now. You should use it and predict his next move.'

'Good idea,' Dan agreed. 'I vote for that.'

Andrew let out a wry laugh. 'Hang on, guys – this isn't something I can control. I can't just click my fingers and enter his mind. The visions are completely unpredictable.'

'Well, have you ever tried?' Tiffany asked pointedly.

'Well, no, but…'

'Then how do you know that you can't?' Poppy said, sitting up.

'I guess it would be pretty cool.' Andrew grinned. He hesitated. 'But even if I could enter his mind, how would I stop him from sensing me?'

'Clear your thoughts completely,' Tiffany said. 'Do not think of anything while you're inside his head. Don't even allow yourself to feel emotion.'

'Not as easy as it sounds,' Andrew said. 'But I'll try.'

He sat back down on the sofa again, letting his arms and legs go floppy. The room fell silent, all except for the hum of nervous breathing, and the slow tick of a clock on Tiffany's mantelpiece. Andrew shut his eyes and let himself drift into a state of deep relaxation, only thinking about one thing…*Vesuvius*.

An explosion of bright white light came out of nowhere, killing the darkness. The sickness he'd felt before was now more intense than ever, churning his insides over and over, as if he was a human washing machine. His head throbbed as he zoomed in and out of consciousness. He finally opened his eyes, expecting to find himself still sitting in Tiffany's living room.

'I don't think it work…' He stopped, suddenly aware of the dark stone walls, with thick green slime growing up them. An overpowering rotten smell drifted through the stale air. And Andrew realised what was happening. He was in the Nightmare Factory…looking out of Vesuvius's eyes.

It *had* worked.

A sudden surge of fear hit him like a tidal wave. *Stop*, Andrew thought. *Got to keep calm. Can't let Vesuvius know I'm here.*

He took a steady breath.

A Shadowmare was standing in front of him. Andrew felt his toes curl. It was a while since he'd been so close to one. The skeletal creature looked up, and its eyes, as red as flaming coals, sent a shiver running down his spine. It had a familiar scar on its left cheek.

There was only one Shadowmare that Andrew knew of that had a scar like that… *Kritchen*, Vesuvius's most trusted servant.

'Master Vesuvius,' Kritchen said in a gruff, scratchy voice. 'It is so good to have you back, sire. It has not been the same without you here. Perhaps now we can continue to—'

'Enough,' Vesuvius interrupted. 'You wanted to speak to me about something?' He was holding his cane, which was crowned with a human skull. He spun it around impatiently in his hand several times. 'And this had better be good, Kritchen. You know I have important work to be doing.'

Kritchen nodded feverishly. 'Yes, Master, of course. You asked us to look for a way of capturing the boy without entering his dreams. Well, I have made an important discovery.'

Vesuvius's slender lips sharpened into a smile.

'And?'

'There is an old law on Earth which states that any demon can cross over to their world on 31st October. It is known as All Hallows Eve, sire, or more commonly, Halloween. It is the day before All Saints' Day.'

'Where did you hear this information, Kritchen? And

74

why have you not brought this to my attention before?'

Stupid, incredulous fool! Andrew heard Vesuvius think.

'We heard it from the spy, sire, at the boy's school. Forgive me, but we've never needed it. We've always stolen children from their dreams quite successfully. But seeing as the boy now owns a dreamcatcher, it is impossible to bring him here using that method.'

'Obviously,' Vesuvius snarled, irritated. 'So tell me more about this... *All Hallows Eve.*'

'There is not much to tell, Master. From the moment darkness falls upon Earth until midnight, a small gap opens up in the veil between worlds, and demons from all over the universe can cross over. If we can find the Releaser within this short window of time and bring him back to the Nightmare Factory, we can generate his fear once again, and release it into the world.'

'And we shall live and rule over the humans once again,' Vesuvius said, letting out a hideous cackle. He lifted a bony finger to his chin. 'Excellent work, Kritchen.' He turned and headed back along the corridor, still laughing to himself.

The boy is mine.

Andrew felt a rush of dread sweep through him...

Halloween was tomorrow.

8

'**D**id it work?'

Andrew opened his eyes.

Relief soared through him. He was back in Tiffany's living room.

'Well?' Tiffany said, eyes shining with excitement. She handed him a cup of tea and knelt in front of him. 'What did you see? Anything important?'

'Oh yes,' Andrew said, a lump growing in his throat. 'It's important alright.'

Dan and Poppy sat either side of him. Jason moved away from the doorway and came and stood in the centre of the room next to Oran.

'I… It's not good,' Andrew said, letting his blond hair flop over his face. 'They can't steal me through my dreams any more so they're going to come for me on Halloween instead.'

'What? But that's tomorrow,' Poppy said, spitting out cookie crumbs everywhere.

'Well, *dur*,' Dan said. 'Anyway, how can they do that? I thought Halloween was just a holiday for getting free sweets. No one actually believes in all that demon rubbish, do they?'

Tiffany jumped up, ignoring Dan. 'That can't be right,' she said, running out into the hallway. She came back moments later carrying a big book entitled *Supernatural 101*. She dumped it on the coffee table and a cloud of grey dust shot out at them, making Andrew sneeze.

'Ha!' Tiffany grinned.

'What?' Dan yanked at her sleeve. 'What does it say?'

'It says that Halloween allows the souls of the *dead* to come back to Earth for one night only.' Her eyes glinted with defiance. 'Well the Shadowmares aren't dead. They won't be able to cross over.'

'Phew,' Poppy said, making a deliberate swipe across her forehead. 'Well then, we're out of the woods.'

'Not necessarily,' Oran said. 'They're Letchians, creatures who survive on the emotions of others, which means they don't have cellular activity or circulatory systems.'

'Huh? In English, please,' Dan said.

'Put it this way. Whilst they're certainly not dead as you and I would understand the word, they're not technically alive either. They may have found a loophole.'

Tiffany threw herself into one of the armchairs.

'You're right. How did we fail to see this before? All these years, and we never even realised.'

'But neither did the Shadowmares,' Andrew pointed out.

'So what's going to happen now?' Jason said. He sounded casual, but his hands were trembling by his sides.

Andrew grinned. 'Bet you wish you'd never got involved, huh?'

Jason shrugged. 'Beats staying in and watching TV, I guess,' he said with a fleeting smile. 'No. It's fine. I'm a part of this now. And I'm going to see it through to the end.'

Tiffany rose from the chair. 'Good. We'll need all the help we can get. We only have to keep Andrew safe for one evening. After that, we're out of the danger zone.'

'You're right.' Oran said. 'And as long as Vesuvius doesn't get hold of Andrew's fear again, the world will remain normal.' He sighed, gripping his unicorn horn tightly in one hand. 'The only thing we have to fear is fear itself.'

'I've heard that somewhere before,' Andrew said.

'Of course you have. It's President Roosevelt, one of the greatest leaders to have lived.'

'Never heard of him,' Dan said. 'So what's the plan?'

'Come straight here after school tomorrow. We can protect each other. Although to be honest with you, I don't think we'll need to. The Shadowmares don't know where Tiffany lives. We should be safe.'

'*Should?*' Andrew said. 'Oran, I love how you fill me with confidence. Although what about Madam Bray? Vesuvius confirmed that she's a spy. She was the one who told them about Halloween.'

Oran put a finger to his lips, as if deep in thought. 'Get a taxi straight from school,' he said. 'And make sure she's not following you.' He reached into his trouser pocket and pulled out a note, handing it to Andrew. 'You can use this.'

'OK, man,' Dan said. 'We can do that.'

'Wait,' Andrew said, studying the money. 'What is this? It looks foreign.' The note had a picture of a colourful bird on one side with a long silver beak. He turned it over. There was a picture of Vesuvius staring back at him.

'Where is this from, Oran?'

'Oops, it's Nusquarium money. I didn't mean to give you that. Wait just a second.' He reached into his other pocket. 'I'm sure I've got some UK currency in here somewhere.'

'You what? Give that here,' Dan said, grabbing it off Andrew. 'Cool, man.'

'What's Nusquarium money?' Jason asked, peering over Dan's shoulder.

'It's what we use in Nusquam to trade with,' Tiffany said. 'The bird is the Fender bird, a creature that according to legend lived in Nusquam many years ago. And Vesuvius... Well, he pretty much dictates everyone and everything in Nusquam nowadays. People are very afraid of him. I doubt they'll be pleased about his return.'

'I didn't know that,' Andrew said, biting his nails.

Oran pulled out a few ten-pound notes. 'Ah, here we go,' he smiled. 'That's more like it.'

'Can I take this?' Dan asked, putting the Nusquam money in his pocket.

Oran smiled. 'Looks like you already did.'

Poppy peered out of the window. 'Come on, Andrew, we'd better get back. Mum doesn't know where we are and it's starting to get dark.'

'Yeah, same,' Jason said. 'Especially with Quentin

Bane all over the news. My parents will be freaking out.'

They walked back into the hallway.

'What a weird day,' Jason said. 'I meet you guys, bunk off school, try and thwart a bank robbery, *and* discover a whole other world I never knew existed.' He paused by the door. 'See you at school then?'

'You betcha,' Andrew said, grinning. 'You won't tell anyone will you?'

'Of course I won't,' Jason said. Then he laughed. 'Mind you I don't think anyone would believe me if I did.'

'True,' Dan said.

They left Tiffany's, fleeing into the chilly autumn air. Jason went one way, and Poppy, Dan and Andrew headed in the other direction towards the tube station.

As they sat in the carriage, seats rattling underneath them, Poppy turned to Andrew, putting a hand on his arm. 'It'll be OK, bro,' she said. 'Vesuvius won't get you this time.'

'I know,' Andrew said. Over the years, he'd got pretty good at putting up a facade, pretending he wasn't afraid of anything, but this time, he couldn't stop the overpowering sense of dread. It was creeping over his body like ivy, spreading with unrelenting ferocity.

What else was Vesuvius planning? There had to be more to this puzzle. Vesuvius wasn't stupid. He'd find Andrew. And when he did, what would happen to everyone else? *Poppy? Dan? Jason? And the rest of the world?* Andrew didn't like the answer to that question.

Later that night, he tossed and turned in his bed. When he finally drifted off to sleep, he dreamt that he was in town, staring up at a blackened sky filled with smoke. Broken glass and rubbish filled the streets. Everything looked as if it had been burned by a terrible fire. It was eerily silent. There were no animals or people in sight.

Andrew spun around as a bone-biting chill enveloped him. The Shadowmares were gliding towards him, arms outstretched. Andrew froze, fear consuming him. Out of the darkness, Vesuvius appeared, taller than ever before. He lifted his skull cane in the air, lips curling into a smile.

'This is the way the world ends, Andrew,' he said.

Then Andrew woke up.

9

The next day at school, Andrew, Poppy, Dan and Jason were sitting in maths class, trying to solve a page of algebra equations. Andrew had only completed one so far, consumed with thoughts about the night ahead. Would Vesuvius capture him again? Would he rule the world like in his nightmare? A chill rushed down his spine. It had felt so real.

'Urgh, this is so boring,' Jason said, pushing his exercise book away.

'I know,' Dan groaned. 'I think my head's about to *explode* with boredom.'

'Only because you're no good at it,' Poppy said, scribbling down what looked like an essay.

'Only because you're a nerd,' Dan muttered, sticking his tongue out playfully at her.

'Andrew, can't you use your powers to help us?' Jason asked.

'What: abracadabra, do my algebra?' Andrew laughed. 'Sorry, Jason, it doesn't work like that.'

There was a knock at the door, and the Head

Teacher's secretary, Mrs Applebee, walked in. Andrew looked up. She was a small, podgy lady, whose skin was ruddy and weathered. Even though she wore heels the size of skyscrapers, she was still shorter than most of the kids in Andrew's class. She whispered something to Mr Sharpe and he nodded.

'You three,' he said, pointing a finger at Dan, Poppy and Andrew. 'Head Teacher's office. Now.'

'Great,' Poppy said, rising from her chair. 'That's never good.'

Dan grabbed Andrew's arm. 'They must have found out about us bunking off school, man. I told you it was a bad idea. And on my first day too – they're going to expel me, I know it.'

'Wouldn't I be called in as well if that were the case?' Jason said. 'I skipped school too, remember?'

'He's got a good point,' Andrew said.

'Silence!' Mr Sharp shouted. 'Stop disrupting the rest of the class.'

'Good luck,' Jason said, giving them a sympathetic smile.

'Thanks,' Andrew said. 'See you at lunch time.'

They followed Mrs Applebee out of the classroom and along the corridor. Her heels clacked against the ground like castanets. They came to a wooden door marked 'Mr Quinn's Office'. Andrew had only ever been here once before, and that was to deliver a note for his Drama teacher.

'Come in,' Mr Quinn said in a slightly aggravated voice. Andrew stepped inside the brightly lit office. It was clean and orderly, with everything aligned along his desk in a neat line. He had sticky labels on almost every item saying things like 'Mr Quinn's stapler' and 'Mr Quinn's ruler'. Even his books were arranged alphabetically on his bookshelf. Somehow, this made Andrew feel even more nervous.

'He's got *way* too much time on his hands,' he muttered.

'Ah,' Mr Quinn said, raising an eyebrow when he saw them. 'Take a seat, please.'

Andrew, Dan and Poppy sat in the three chairs placed in front of his desk.

'So,' Dan said, smiling. 'Why did you ask us here, sir?'

'You can wipe that grin off your face right now Mr…' He paused, running his finger down a list of names. 'Mr Bage,' he said. 'My secretary informs me that yesterday was your first day. Why were you not at school?'

Dan groaned quietly and sank into his chair. 'I told you we were in trouble,' he whispered to Andrew.

'I… We…' Andrew faltered. 'How did you find out, sir?'

'Does it matter?' Mr Quinn said. 'The point is that you were skipping school.'

'Can you prove it?'

'I beg your pardon?' His face grew fiercely red, as if he was being pumped up with air. 'Young man, you are treading on very thin ice. One of the dinner ladies saw you leaving the school premises and we have it on CCTV. If you question my authority once more I will have to take serious action.'

'Yes, sir,' Andrew said.

'Sir, it was an emergency,' Poppy said. 'Our aunt… she's in hospital. Her name's Tiffany Grey. I can give you her number and you can telephone her if you—'

'That won't be necessary, Miss Lake, thank you. I'm sure it took you a very long time to come up with that story but I have already spoken to your parents and neither of them had any idea that you weren't in school. As your Head Teacher, it is my obligation to make sure you are safe, and if you disobey our rules, you must be punished. Therefore, you will join Mrs Simmons at four pm for three hours of detention, which I have already agreed with your parents.'

'Three hours?' Andrew said. 'After school? Today?'

'Yes. You'll miss the Halloween dance. Will that be a problem?' Mr Quinn asked.

'Well, sir, it's just—'

'Because if it is, I can arrange for a permanent transfer to another school if you'd prefer—'

'No,' Poppy interrupted. 'Four pm... That'll be fine, sir. Thank you.'

They got up and walked out of the office, not saying another word until they reached the corridor.

'*Thank you*?' Andrew said, raising an eyebrow. 'He was giving us detention, not handing out chocolate bars.'

'I was trying to save your butt from being kicked out of school,' Poppy growled. 'And if you ask me, we're getting off pretty lightly. Usually they expel kids for this kind of thing.'

'Why did you ask for proof?' Dan said. 'That wound him right up.'

Andrew leant against the wall, sighing. 'I was trying to find out if Madam Bray was behind this. Turns out I was right. She wanted us to have detention tonight. Hell, I bet she even suggested it.'

Dan rolled his eyes. 'Of course she suggested it. She hates us.'

'Actually, I don't think that's what Andrew meant,' Poppy said.

'It wasn't?'

Andrew shook his head. 'Sure, she hates us, but there's more to it than that. She needs us here to keep a close eye on us. She knows we're not stupid enough to show up to the Halloween ball, so she planned this. Detention. Now when Vesuvius comes, she can lead him directly to us.'

Dan's eyes widened. 'Oh, God, you're right. So what do we do?'

'I'm not sure,' Andrew said. 'If you get any genius brainwaves, let me know.' He walked in front of them, his mind buzzing with worry. What would he do? He could either skip detention and risk being expelled, or go to detention and risk Vesuvius finding him. It wasn't exactly an easy choice to make.

At lunch time, they headed to the cafeteria. The mood was still tense. Poppy stood in the lunch queue biting on her nails, while Dan seemed to be deep in thought.

'Why do you think she didn't tell on me?' Jason said, picking up four trays from the pile and handing them out.

Andrew took one and placed it under his arm.

'I dunno, I guess she doesn't have a problem with you.'

Madam Bray eyed them coldly as they moved further up the queue.

'Is she really that spiteful?' Jason said. 'That she'd purposely try and get you in trouble, just because she dislikes you?'

Dan let out a loud snort.

'Yes,' Andrew said. 'Believe me. She is.'

They reached the counter. Madam Bray was stood serving up food to kids, but something was different about her. Andrew didn't know what, but it gave him the creeps. She seemed to be smiling a lot more, laughing and joking with the other dinner ladies like she'd been there forever. But behind the fake smile, there was hatred in her eyes. A deep, poisonous hatred.

She snarled when she saw them.

'You should stay away from these nasty little children,' she said to Jason. 'They'll get you into trouble.'

Jason shrugged, looking uncomfortable. He opened his mouth to say something but before he had the chance Andrew pushed in front of him.

'Why are you here?' he said bluntly. Madam Bray's head snapped around. A small smile slid over her lips. 'What do you mean? This is my job.'

'You know what he means,' Poppy said, coming up from behind Andrew and folding her arms. 'You hate children. Especially us.'

'Yeah,' Dan said. 'What's the deal?'

Madam Bray carried on spooning the food onto their trays. 'I have my reasons,' she said mysteriously.

Yeah, I bet you do, thought Andrew.

'Carrots or peas?' Madam Bray asked.

'Neither,' Andrew growled, pulling his tray away. He began to walk away, but Madam Bray called him back. 'Andrew?'

'Now what?'

'Things are changing. Vesuvius is coming back. I'd be very careful if I were you. Try to stop him and you could end up getting very hurt.'

'Really?' Andrew said, putting the tray down. 'Is that a threat?' His fists were clenched into tight balls. He could feel the power running through his veins, and he had to battle with himself not to use it on Madam Bray.

'Come on,' Poppy whispered, grabbing him by the arm. 'She's not worth it.' Andrew took a deep breath. She was right. He couldn't risk exposing his powers in front of all these people.

Poppy led him away to a table at the back of the

cafeteria. He flung himself down onto one of the chairs, letting out an angry sigh. 'That woman needs a brain check,' he said, kicking the table leg with his shoe. 'Why is she still on his side? After everything that he's done to her?'

'She's crazy,' Poppy said. 'We discovered that long ago.'

Jason stayed silent, looking down at the table.

'What's got into you?' Dan said.

He shrugged, shoving a forkful of peas into his mouth. 'Oh, nothing. Just nervous about tonight.'

'We all are,' Poppy said.

'It'll be fine,' Dan said, biting into his pizza slice. 'As long as we keep Andrew safe, Vesuvius doesn't stand a chance.'

Jason looked up. 'But what if something goes wrong?' His brown eyes were wide and unblinking. 'What if Vesuvius manages to capture Andrew again? It's going to be pitch black outside once you get out of detention.'

'Maybe we should get word to Oran,' Poppy said.

'Don't worry,' Andrew told them 'Maybe we can get out early or something, before it gets too dark.'

'I'll come up with something,' Jason said with a smile. He shuffled in his chair. 'But I need to know.

What would happen if Vesuvius caught you? He'd take you back to the Nightmare Factory and extract your fear, but then what?'

'Well,' Andrew said, 'he'd unleash it into the world. Nightmares would become real. I mean, really real. People's fears would come to life. And Shadowmares would rule the Earth.'

Jason pushed his tray away with a trembling hand. 'I think I've lost my appetite.'

'Can I have your pudding?' Dan asked, pulling Jason's tray towards him and helping himself.

Detention was moving painfully slowly. The music boomed from the assembly hall across the playground. Every now and then Andrew would hear screams of children outside, racing around, having fun. They had no idea of the danger that loomed over them. Time seemed to drag. Andrew stared at the clock on the wall, every second feeling like an hour. He just wanted to get out of here, and go to Tiffany's house where they would be safe.

He'd read everything from the posters on the wall to the sign on the door warning students to walk, not run, in an attempt to try and forget about Vesuvius.

He glanced over at Poppy and Dan, who were sitting on separate tables. Poppy was busy biting her nails. Dan was scratching something into the desk. One of their teachers, Mrs Simmons, a short woman with ginger hair, was overseeing the detention. She sat on a chair at the front of the class room, reading a book and occasionally poking her nose up over the pages at them.

Andrew glanced at the clock again. *5.30 pm.* It was nearly dark outside. They had to get out before Vesuvius crossed over to Earth.

A deafening noise rang through the air. *The fire alarm.* Even now, after everything that had happened, Andrew still stiffened at the sound. All the kids rose from their chairs, looking around at each other, not knowing what to do.

'Everybody outside,' Mrs Simmons said calmly, shooing them out of the class room. 'Form an orderly line in the playground. I'm going to find out what this is all about.'

They tumbled out of the door, fifteen of them in total, all shouting over the noise of the alarm. A sweet smell of candyfloss and toffee apples filled the air as kids from the dance flooded out of the hall opposite. They were all wearing masks and carrying jack-o'-lanterns. Some were dressed as witches with

93

tall pointed hats, others wore mummy costumes or were dressed as their favourite horror-movie villains. Andrew usually loved Halloween. It was his favourite night of the year. But not tonight. Not tonight.

Andrew felt someone grab him by the shoulder. He flinched, spinning around. A white face with fierce black eyes stared back at him. For a moment, Andrew felt his heart shoot up into his throat.

Jason peeled his mask off, grinning underneath. 'The alarm was a good idea, huh?'

'That was you?' Andrew whispered.

'Yeah, I said I'd think of something, didn't I? Come on, hurry up, Mrs Simmons will be back soon. If we go now, I doubt she'll even notice you're gone.' He handed them a mask each. 'Picked these up for you.' He grinned.

They put them on. 'Genius, man!' Dan said.

'It's almost dark,' Poppy said, glancing at the sky. 'We'd better get a move on. Vesuvius will be here soon.'

Just as she had spoken these words, a terrifying scream filled the air. The crowd parted. Some children were scurrying to get away. Others were pointing and shouting.

'Wow, look at him,' one kid said. 'What an awesome costume!'

Andrew stepped forward, eager to see what all the fuss was about. That was when he noticed dark shadows creeping up out of every corner, filling the quad with a terrible blackness. Vesuvius stepped out, his frail figure towering over everything, black eyes locked right on Andrew.

10

Andrew stood frozen to the spot. Even in his mask, Vesuvius still knew it was him. 'Run!' Jason shouted. Andrew raced up the steps into the corridor. He turned briefly and saw Vesuvius gaining on them.

'Your powers!' Poppy screamed. 'Use them.'

Andrew nodded, but didn't stop running. He pointed his finger at Vesuvius and a beam of light shot out. Vesuvius dodged it, faster than a bullet.

He cackled and held his skull cane up, firing back a stream of purple rays. Andrew felt something hot pierce his shoulder.

'Ouch!' he screamed. The pain radiated along his arm, burning through his flesh. He glanced down. His school uniform had melted away and his skin was raw and weeping. Everything was a blur; his head was spinning.

'In here,' Jason said, beckoning him over. He was leaning out of a doorway. Andrew hurried inside with Poppy and Dan. It was dark. There was barely enough room to move a muscle. From what he could make out, they were in what looked like a caretaker's cupboard. There were mops and cleaning fluids and vacuum cleaners spilling out from the shelves.

'Keep quiet until Vesuvius leaves,' Jason whispered.

'He's not going to leave,' Andrew said.

'Maybe if we wait in here long enough he will. You're hardly in a fit state to fight,' Poppy said.

An icy hand reached out from within the shadows. Andrew flinched, spinning around to see a pair of glowing red eyes staring back at him.

At first he thought it was more kids in costumes, but the coldness was too intense.

'*Shadowmares. In the cupboard,*' he managed to croak, seeing his own breath.

Poppy, Dan and Jason screamed. Andrew flung the door open, but Vesuvius was waiting outside, grinning widely with a crooked smile that exposed his rotten teeth.

'Come,' he hissed, as he wrapped his cloak around Andrew, embracing him in a frosty grasp. Coldness filled his bones, chilling his blood, as darkness crashed over him like a gaping mouth swallowing him up.

11

Andrew coughed at the putrid smell of mould and stale air. He felt a fierce pain at the back of his neck. His eyes snapped open. Terror seized him, ripping through his body.

He was back in the Nightmare Factory.

He gazed around at the brick walls, covered in thick green slime. There were no windows. It was like being trapped in a large box. He was lying on a wooden bed with no mattress. There was a grimy toilet and sink in one corner, plastered with rust. It was exactly how he remembered – only this time, he didn't have Poppy with him for support. Maybe that was a good thing. She was safe back at home, or at least she would be until they extracted Andrew's fear and released it into the world again. He had to stop them. Somehow, he had to escape.

How long had he been here? Minutes? Hours? There was no way of knowing.

His head was throbbing like it had its own heartbeat. He reached around his shoulder, and sure enough, his hand found a metal disc no bigger than a two-pound coin. Of course: *a fear plug*. It was what the Shadowmares used to plug kids into the Fear Pods in order to extract their fear.

The metal door rattled against its frame. Andrew jumped down from the bed and scurried to the back of the room, putting up his hands, ready to blast whoever came through the door. It crashed open, revealing two Shadowmares hovering in midair, red eyes burning in their long milk-coloured skulls. Their cloaks, crafted from shadows, swayed as if being blown by a gentle wind.

'Stay back,' Andrew said.

The Shadowmares drifted closer towards him. Andrew felt his palms growing hot. The warmth radiated from his fingers and came bursting out in shafts of purple light, hitting the Shadowmares square in their chests. They collapsed to the ground.

'Yes!' Andrew said, punching the air, but then more Shadowmares appeared through the doorway, and the coldness became unbearable. They tumbled inside like a waterfall of smoke. All at once, they opened their jaws up into black pits and breathed frosty air over Andrew. The rush of cold smacked his skin with all the force of a truck. He staggered backwards, his limbs frozen as if his blood was turning to ice. The Shadowmares swept towards him and lifted him by the scruff of his neck.

He fell in and out of consciousness as he was dragged through the dimly-lit corridors, deeper and deeper underground. The brightness of the hall tugged him back to reality. It was deathly silent. His eyes flitted to the wall of skulls, of children who had long ago disobeyed Vesuvius and paid the price with their lives. They glowed eerily in the artificial lights, like pearls in the sun.

He shivered. Perhaps that would be his fate.

The Shadowmares let go of him and he fell to the cold marble floor like a rag doll, watching helplessly as they began to turn the huge metal cogs attached to the fireplace. He knew what was behind it, but he was almost too weak to care. Slowly, the fireplace slid back to reveal a pool of blackness.

'Up,' Kritchen hissed. 'Through there. Into the Dark Room.'

Andrew flinched at the words. They brought back terrifying memories. The Dark Room was where the Fear Pods were kept. It was where Vesuvius had first discovered Andrew's fear of fire and had used it to create nightmares all over the world.

He got to his feet, muscles aching, and the Shadowmares dragged him into the darkness. Hundreds of fiery embers stared back at him.

A light flashed on, blinding Andrew with its intensity. He screwed his eyes shut, and could still see the Shadowmares' faces, as if their glowing skulls had been burned onto his retina.

The room was immense, as big as a football stadium. But instead of seats, there were rows of Fear Pods. They were exactly as Andrew remembered – big glass domes with a seat and a helmet inside them. Dozens of snake-like wires sprouted out of them, which were all attached to the central fear cylinder in the middle of the Dark Room.

'Welcome back,' a familiar voice said. Andrew turned to see Vesuvius towering over him. He tapped his skull cane on the floor, as if deep in thought. 'I wonder what your fear is this time?' He stepped closer, lifting his bony fingers and running them down Andrew's cheek. His touch was like ice. Andrew clenched his teeth, fighting the pain.

'Get off me. You're not going to have my fear. Not this time, Vesuvius. Not ever again.'

Vesuvius cackled. 'Oh, but I will. In fact, I already have a pretty good idea of what it could be.'

101

Was he tricking him? Andrew didn't even know what he was afraid of. So how could Vesuvius?

The Shadowmares grabbed Andrew again and dragged him to the nearest Fear Pod. Vesuvius followed, watching keenly. The glass door sprang open and Andrew was forced inside. As soon as he sat down the wires twisted around him, pinning his arms and legs down. Andrew struggled, and the wires pulled tighter around his skin.

There was a buzzing sound from above, and slowly the helmet moved down over his head.

'Oh, and don't try to use your powers this time,' Vesuvius spat. 'I've had the Fear Pod reinforced with special glass so any efforts to break free will be futile.'

Special glass? thought Andrew. What did he mean? Did that even exist? If Vesuvius was telling the truth, he was doomed. His only hope was to blank out all thoughts, or pray for Oran to come and save him…

'Goodbye, Andrew,' Vesuvius said, and with a flap of his cloak, he turned and headed for the door.

The lights flashed off and Andrew was plunged into darkness again. Hundreds of glowing red eyes appeared from the gloom and floated towards him. Thick black tentacles crept out of the Shadowmares' cloaks. They crawled through the holes in the pod, wrapping their icy, wet limbs around Andrew like giant slugs. Andrew braced himself. He knew what was coming. The coldness exploded into his skull, as they pushed their shadowy tentacles through the fear plug and into his brain.

For a moment, Andrew turned numb. He gasped for air, lungs convulsing.

'Get out of my brain.'

'Not until we find your fear,' Kritchen said with a cruel smile.

Andrew shut his eyes. He didn't want to give the Shadowmares any insight into his mind. He needed to block his thoughts out somehow. What was the most boring, monotonous thing he could think of? Maths? Yes, he would do sums in his head. The seven times table.

Seven, fourteen, twenty-one, twenty-eight, thirty-five, he counted. *Forty-two, forty-nine…* It wasn't working. He could feel the coldness running through every part of his brain. He could feel the Shadowmares sorting through his memories as if they were raiding through rubbish in a skip.

'I can see fire,' Kritchen said. 'But that's an old fear, isn't it? What else do you have in here?' His voice was gutteral, like a dying man taking his last breath. 'What are you afraid of now, Andrew? Let's try something else.' He began slowly transforming into a man with no skin, with red-raw flesh and grisly intestines bursting from his stomach as if he was inside out. He had no lips, just spiky teeth that looked like pitchforks wedged together. All of the other Shadowmares in the Dark Room started to change into the revolting skinless creature too. Andrew laughed. It was a villain from one of his many horror movies. But it wasn't scary...

'No? Not your fear?' Kritchen said, as if he wasn't surprised. 'OK, let's try again...'

For what seemed like days but was probably only hours, Kritchen and the other Shadowmares read Andrew's brain. They shape-shifted into every different monster they could find in his imagination, from every single horror film he'd ever seen. Andrew's muscles twanged with exhaustion. His head throbbed.

There was a knock on the Fear Pod, dragging him from his half-asleep, half-awake state back to reality. Vesuvius stood looking down at him, mouth twisted like he'd just bitten into a lemon.

'Feed him,' Vesuvius said.

A small hatch in the pod opened up, and Kritchen

104

shoved a tray with a glass of water and two plain crackers through it, placing it on Andrew's lap. They were weakening him so that they could read his mind, but they still needed to keep him alive if they wanted to find his fear.

'Eat,' Vesuvius said.

The hatch closed. The wires loosened from around Andrew's arms. He stretched the cramp out of them, and then looked longingly down at the crackers. His stomach grumbled, willing him to eat. Andrew laughed dryly, and tossed it aside, water and food running down the glass dome. He felt a sharp pang in his stomach, as if it was protesting.

Vesuvius snarled. A surge of power raced through Andrew. He was back in control.

His dry lips managed a smile. 'I would rather… die…before…you find…my fear.'

'Oh, you'll die,' Vesuvius said bitterly. 'Make no mistake: when I have your fear, you'll all die. Your mother, your friends, your dearest twin, Poppy, everyone that you ever cared about will die, *just like your father*'

The words sent a wave of anger through Andrew. 'No,' he shouted. 'I won't let you touch them. I won't let you near them.' Just the pure thought caused an ocean of fear to bubble up inside him. He lifted his arms up and projected a stream of light at Vesuvius, but it hit the edges of the glass pod, bouncing off and evaporating into thin air.

'I warned you,' Vesuvius hissed.

Andrew felt tears rolling down his cheeks. He didn't want to cry in front of Vesuvius, didn't want to appear weak, but he felt overwhelmed with dread, like it was seeping out from his very soul. What if the others died because of him?

Vesuvius smiled suddenly, black eyes twinkling in the dark. He reached over and whispered something into Kritchen's ear.

'Yes, Master.' Kritchen nodded. 'I'll try that now.'

What would he try? Andrew asked himself. He'd given up blocking the Shadowmares out. It was useless. They were too strong. He watched as images were forced into his head. Images too powerful to ignore. Demons and beasts running through the streets. Buildings in ruins, shops burnt down. Vesuvius laughing, head rolling back and cackling like a madman in the chaos of it all. Poppy crying; Dan, Oran, Jason, Tiffany, his mother, being tortured by Shadowmares. Children hurt. More crying. More screaming.

Then Andrew realised that he was screaming too.

His throat was dry. His cheeks were wet with tears.

'Who would have guessed?' Vesuvius said, eyes blazing defiantly. 'The thing you are most afraid of… is *me.*'

Andrew swallowed back tears. 'Not you, Vesuvius. You'll never scare me.' He didn't want to give him that satisfaction. 'It's what you're capable of doing with my fear which worries me. You're going to destroy the entire world.'

Vesuvius nodded. 'And it's all thanks to you.'

Tears flowed easily. There was no point in stopping them. Vesuvius was right about one thing – it was all his fault.

Andrew closed his eyes, weary from too much crying. Hungry. Worn out. He could feel the fear being sucked from him like water down a plughole. His throat was so dry he could barely swallow. The weight of what he'd done hung over him, crushing him with dread. He welcomed the thought of dying now. Leaving all the guilt and the fear and the pain behind…

Hours, days, weeks passed without Andrew giving much thought to anything at all. He was drifting in and out of consciousness, too weak to determine what was reality and what was just a nightmare.

'Andrew.'

The voice stirred him. His eyes shot open. Oran was standing next to the pod, giant hands pressed up against the glass. His long white hair trailed over his shoulders. His blue eyes were surrounded by thick, dark circles and they had lost much of their sparkle. Surely it was just another hallucination? Oran couldn't be here. Kritchen was shape-shifting again, playing tricks on Andrew's mind.

He shut his eyes, too drained to respond.

'Andrew,' the voice said again. 'Wake up.'

Andrew blinked several times. 'Oran? Is that really you?'

The tall figure in green nodded, and then grinned.

'I'm going to get you out of here.'

'Water,' Andrew croaked.

'Later. We need to hurry. I don't think it'll be long before the Shadowmares come back.'

Andrew nodded, watching as Oran pushed a button on the side of the pod. The glass door sprang open automatically. Oran climbed inside, clutching a knife. He leant over and cut the wires which were holding Andrew down. They coiled and spat as if they were alive.

'Can you stand?'

Andrew tried getting to his feet, but his legs collapsed like a house of cards.

'Never mind,' Oran said. He lifted Andrew over his shoulder, and carried him through the Dark Room. They passed several lifeless Shadowmares slumped on the ground. Had Oran killed them to rescue him? Andrew felt himself being lifted out into the coolness of the main corridor. He shut his eyes again, too exhausted to think. Within seconds, he was asleep.

Andrew awoke in a room with white walls and a table, which looked a bit like a spaceship. The groggy, dizzy feeling slowly drifted away and he realised he was slouched in one of the egg-shaped chairs in Oran's dining room. He stretched out, yawning, running his toes through a carpet which felt as soft and fluffy as cotton wool. He rubbed his eyes, glancing up.

'Ah, you've come round,' Oran smiled, passing him a glass of water.

'Thanks,' Andrew said, taking the glass and downing it in one go. He paused. 'How long was I in the Dark Room for?'

'Three weeks,' Oran said. 'I tried to rescue you sooner but Vesuvius has been on constant watch.'

He handed Andrew another glass of water, which he sipped thirstily.

'Where is he now?' Andrew said, looking around apprehensively.

'He's…' Oran paused. 'A lot has happened since he managed to get your fear. Let me make you some food and I'll explain everything. You must be starving.'

Andrew's stomach grumbled at the mention of food.

'Yeah,' he said. 'Actually, I am.'

Oran crossed over to the Satebite oven in the corner, which looked a bit like a satellite dish suspended over a hob. Andrew had seen him cook with it before, although he wasn't exactly sure how it worked. He knew that if you put a picture of food underneath the Satebite, seconds later it would appear as real food, as if from thin air.

Oran took out a photo album. It was full of pictures of all different kinds of cuisines. 'What do you fancy?'

'Anything,' Andrew said. 'I'm so hungry I could eat a horse right now.'

Oran scratched his head. 'Hmm. I don't think I have a picture of a horse. Let me go and check with one of the Luguarna men.' He turned, walking towards the door.

'It was just an expression,' Andrew said, laughing. 'I don't really want a horse. Just give me whatever.'

'Oh.' Oran smiled. 'Bangers and mash it is, then.' He placed a picture underneath the Satebite. There was a buzzing sound and a bright flash of light, and then a plate of steaming hot sausages and mash appeared on top of the picture.

'Cool!' Andrew said. The smell of gravy drifted up his nose, making his mouth water uncontrollably. Oran handed him a knife and fork, then sat back down in the opposite chair.

'So,' he said, putting his hands together and looking serious. 'Vesuvius has your fear again. And lots of it.'

'I'm so sorry,' Andrew said, through a mouthful of mashed potatoes. 'I tried to hide it from him, but I was too weak.'

'It's not your fault. Once he had you back, it seemed almost inevitable. Now we must try and deal with the consequences. As I said, he has already started releasing it into the world. And I'm not going to lie, Andrew; it's bad. Really bad.'

Andrew stopped chewing and looking up. 'How bad?'

'The world is in chaos. The Shadowmares are pretty much ruling everything now. Schools, shops, banks, they're all closed.' Andrew felt suddenly sick. 'Vesuvius has huge amounts of your fear. It's enough to last him a century…possibly more. And that's not all – Vesuvius has these plants set up all over the place. He calls them Fear Farms.'

'Fear Farms?' Andrew gasped.

'Yes. They're full of Fear Pods. He's got humans locked up in them like cattle. And he has Shadowmares guarding them around the clock so that no one can escape.' Oran paused, gazing at his feet. 'Andrew… they've captured Tiffany. And your mother too. I'm so sorry.'

'What?' Andrew jumped up. His legs were still weak but he managed to stay standing. 'We need to go and save them.'

'I know,' Oran said. 'But are you sure you're feeling up to it? You can stay here for another day, rest until your energy returns and then—'

'No,' Andrew said. 'I'm fine now I've had something to eat. Come on, we need to get going. How do we get to the Sliders room from here?' The Sliders room was what Oran used to transport kids back to Earth. Oran had used it to get them home once before.

'The Sliders room is for people stolen from their dreams,' Oran said. 'But this time you're here in

112

your physical body so we can use one of the portals, which will be quicker. Come here,' he said, beckoning Andrew over to the rug.

'Is it a magic carpet? Andrew asked.

Oran laughed, holding his belly. 'Good heavens, no. I've just got it there to mark where the portal is.'

'OK,' Andrew said, stepping gingerly onto the rug. 'So how does this happen?'

'Close your eyes,' Oran said. 'Now, I want you to think of Hyde Park. Have you been there before?' Andrew nodded. 'Good. Concentrate on going there and say the magic words with me. "Aska Babaka, Nusquam arrow. Take me to where I want to go."'

Andrew opened his eyes. 'What? You've got to be joking, right?'

'Not at all.' Oran smiled. 'It comes from an ancient Nusquarium language. It means "Portal that I stand upon". Trust me, it'll work.'

'Alright, if you say so…' He shut his eyes again, and together they said the words.

'*Aska Babaka, Nusquam arrow. Take me to where I want to go.*'

Andrew hurtled through a tunnel of bright light, spinning like a Frisbee.

He tumbled onto what felt like soft wet grass.

'Ouch,' he said, rubbing his head. He sat up and peered around. He was in a park, but the grass and the trees were blackened and dead-looking, as if burned by a terrible fire. There was a bench beside him, which looked out over a small lake. He gasped. The water was a putrid red colour, like blood…

What the hell? He sat down on the bench, head spinning with confusion. Had he transported himself to another world by accident? What if he was lost and could never get home again?

'Hello,' Oran smiled, appearing beside him.

Andrew jumped. 'God, Oran, you almost gave me a heart attack. Where are we?'

'Don't you recognise it? It's Hyde Park.'

'*This* is Hyde Park?' Andrew said, staring around.

'I warned you that things had changed a little.'

'A little?' Andrew said. 'It looks like it got a makeover from hell.'

'Well, it kind of did.'

The surface of the scarlet water bubbled vigorously as a monstrous green creature rose up out of the lake. It had thick slimy skin sagging off its back like seaweed. Oran tugged Andrew back off the bench as a sweeping giant tentacle ploughed towards them. They sprinted up the hill, only stopping to turn around when they were sure they were out of reach.

'What was that thing?' Andrew gasped, catching his breath.

'No idea,' Oran said. 'A monster from someone's nightmare. London's full of strange creatures at the moment. Let's get out of here.'

They ran out of Hyde Park and into Knightsbridge. This part of town was usually full of posh businessmen in suits and ladies with fur coats and designer handbags, but right now it was completely deserted. The store windows had all been smashed in, and their contents looted. Shattered glass littered the street. Andrew watched as a group of teenage lads came running out of Harvey Nichols carrying a flatscreen TV. Shop and car alarms were blaring, sending a deafening cry over the city.

'Where are all the police?' Andrew said.

'There are none. Some of them tried to maintain order at first, but they've all been captured and put in Fear Farms now. The rest are too afraid to do anything,' Oran said. He sighed, holding his unicorn horn tightly in one hand. 'Fear breeds chaos.'

'Roosevelt again?' Andrew asked.

'No, that one I made up myself.'

A pang of fear twisted in his stomach. 'Where are the others?'

'I told them to wait in the cafe up the road. They've collected a few kids who they found wandering the streets. Kids who have lost their parents and have nowhere to go. Poppy's been cooking for them and Dan and Jason have been taking it in turns to guard the place.'

Andrew nodded. He couldn't believe how bad things had got. Kids…homeless, hungry. All alone. It wasn't right.

He slumped down on the kerb, feeling defeated. His head felt hot. His hands were clammy. He wanted to crawl into a hole and never return. 'I can't do this any more,' he said, trying not to cry. 'This is all my fault. Vesuvius has the entire world in the palm of his hand. Tiffany and Mum could end up dying because of me. Everyone could…' He choked up, unable to finish.

Oran took a deep breath and sat down beside him.

'Listen, Andrew, there's something I've learned very recently and it's that you can't change life. What will happen, will happen. You just have to face your fear and jump in for the ride. So what will it be? Are you going to stay here and ruminate about what could go wrong? Or are you going to face your fear like a true hero?'

Andrew thought about this. He supposed Oran was right. Sitting here crying about it wasn't going to change things.

'How far?' Andrew said, standing up.

Oran smiled. 'Five minutes. We're nearly there.'

A couple of kids raced past them, pushing Andrew into the wall. Seconds later, more people came running from the same direction.

Andrew grabbed one of them by the arm. He was a teenager, maybe sixteen or seventeen at the most.

'What is it? Who's out there?'

The boy stared at Andrew, eyes glossy with terror.

'A-an-army,' he stuttered, pointing round the corner. He broke away from Andrew's grasp and began running down the street again.

'What's he talking about?' Andrew said. 'Why's he scared of the army? Surely it's a good thing they're here?'

A low rumbling noise echoed against the surrounding buildings, making the ground under their feet shake like an earthquake.

Stones and rubbish danced on the pavement. The grumbling sound got louder. A tank turned into the street, monstrous-looking, like the ones Andrew had seen in Second World War movies. He felt a wave of nausea crash over him as the huge chunk of metal ploughed towards them. And Andrew realised with a sudden rush of panic that he was staring straight down the barrel of its gun…

12

'Aim, fire!' shouted the soldier manning the turret of the tank.

Andrew threw himself sideways just as the tank blasted a hole the size of a bus into the designer handbag shop behind him. The noise from the explosion was deafening, and for a few moments afterwards, all Andrew could hear was ringing in his ears. A cloud of dust filled the air, spreading the smell of burnt leather. When it had cleared, he saw that the tank had turned and was about to fire another shell into a fish restaurant. There was a high-pitched shattering noise as the window broke into a million pieces, sending fragments of glass raining down on them.

'I don't understand. Why is the army destroying our city?'

'It's not the army,' Oran said, taking cover in a doorway. 'They're soldiers straight out of someone's nightmare. And it seems like they're hellbent on destroying everything in sight.' He pointed to a small restaurant with a grubby yellow sign above it saying *Coco's*. 'Hurry! Over there!' he said.

Andrew peered curiously at the building. It looked familiar. Then he realised why. He'd been there as a kid, with Poppy and Mum, only back then it had been quaint-looking and always busy. Now it sat lonely and abandoned, the 'Open' sign hanging haphazardly from the cracked window.

They hurried inside. The cafe was full of tables and chairs. The broken ones had been stacked up against the walls. The floor had been recently mopped, and the place smelt of disinfectant. Andrew laughed. Despite everything, Poppy was cleaning. He shouldn't have expected anything less.

'Andrew!' Dan yelled, running up to him. 'I thought you were a goner, mate.'

'Yeah, me too,' Andrew said with a grin.

'Hiya, Andrew,' Jason said, appearing from the back. 'I'm glad you're OK.'

'Thanks. You too.' Their clothes and hair were grubby, and they had a few scratches on them, but apart from that they looked fine. 'Where's Poppy?'

'Downstairs. She's just put the kids to bed.'

'How many are there?'

'About twenty of them. Most of their parents are

either dead or locked up in Fear Farms. Poppy insisted that we look after them, stop them from getting captured as well. I suppose it's for the best, really.'

Their parents had been killed? Andrew felt his throat tighten. He'd caused all of this, and somehow he needed to put things right.

Andrew paced up and down. 'We need to free everyone from the Fear Farms. Perhaps then we can form an army or something. You know, start a revolution.' It was optimistic, but Andrew couldn't see any other way out of this mess. They wouldn't be able to fight Vesuvius alone.

Dan nodded. 'We were thinking along those lines too. We're got some stuff to show you. Come on, let's go and get Poppy.'

Andrew followed them down the steep steps. The downstairs part of the restaurant did not have much light, but it was perfect for hiding out in. Poppy had laid out blankets and blow-up beds on the floor for the children to sleep on.

'Where did you get all of this bedding from?' Andrew asked.

'I got it from the camping shop down the road,' Dan said.

Andrew raised an eyebrow. 'You mean you stole it?'

'No, of course not. I just borrowed it.'

'Borrowed?' Andrew said. 'You can't borrow from a shop.'

'Why not?' Dan said, his voice slightly higher pitched than usual. 'I'm going to take it all back. And besides, we need this stuff to survive. It's not like I went looting designer gear like everybody else.'

'*Shh!* You'll wake the children,' Poppy hissed, coming out of the bathroom. 'Andrew!' she said, running up to him and throwing her arms around him. 'I'm so glad you're OK.'

Several of the kids moaned and stirred.

'Come on,' she whispered, pointing upstairs. They tiptoed back up to the main part of the restaurant, and sat down at one of the tables.

'Mum's in one of the Fear Farms…and Tiffany too,' Poppy said. Her nose twitched as if she was about to burst into tears.

'I know,' Andrew sighed. 'But you've done really well. Looking after all of these kids on your own… Mum would be proud.'

Poppy looked up, smiling. 'You think so?'

'Definitely.' Andrew said. He turned to the others. 'So what's the plan?'

Jason took out a map from his pocket and laid it

flat on the table. 'This is the layout of Piccadilly tube station. It's where we think Tiffany and your mum are being kept.'

'What?' Andrew said. 'In a tube station?'

'Yes,' Oran said. 'All the Fear Farms are situated underground. We believe the Shadowmares like it there because it's dark. They spend their days in the tube stations, feeding and sleeping, and then come up into the streets at night.'

Andrew nodded slowly. 'I suppose that makes sense. So if we go there now, there should be fewer of them to stop us?'

'That's the plan,' Dan said. 'Whether it'll work or not…'

Andrew walked over to the window and peeled back the blinds. None of the street lamps were on, but the moon cast a pale glow over the city. 'OK,' he said. 'Grab some torches.'

'We're going now?' Poppy said.

'We need to start getting people out of there. The longer we leave them in the Fear Pods, the weaker they'll get,' Andrew said. 'Believe me, I know.'

'But what about the kids? We can't just leave them here alone.'

'Why not?' Dan said. 'They're asleep. They'll be fine.'

The room began to shake, throwing them off their chairs.

'OK, they *were* asleep.'

Dust and rubble fell from the ceiling, covering them in a thick, white powder. 'What's happening?' Andrew shouted over the noise of collapsing concrete.

'Earthquake,' Oran said. 'We've had a few of them recently but this one's definitely the worst yet.'

'Earthquake? In London? You've got to be kidding, right?'

Oran shook his head. 'Andrew, anything is possible now Vesuvius has begun releasing your fear. Even a full-blown avalanche.'

There was another rumble and the whole building shook violently.

'Don't tempt fate,' Dan said wryly.

The sound of crying came from downstairs as more and more dust began to fall from the ceiling. Andrew grabbed the table, steadying himself.

A kid appeared at the top of the stairs. He looked about ten, with glasses and short blond hair. 'What's going on?' he said. 'The toddlers are screaming the house down.'

'Another earthquake,' Poppy said. 'I'll be down in a second. Get them to hide under the tables.'

'We've got to go now.' Andrew said. 'Things are getting worse. If we leave it any longer, there won't be a world left to protect.'

'He's right,' Jason said. 'It's now or never.'

Poppy hesitated, biting down hard on her lip. 'OK.' she turned to the boy. 'Allen, can you look after the kids while I'm gone? Get the older ones to help change nappies and feed them and stuff. We're going to be a while so I'm putting you in charge.'

Allen nodded, puffing out his chest. 'Sure thing,' he said. 'I can keep them safe.'

'OK, good,' Oran said. 'That's decided then. Poppy, go and get the weapons.'

Poppy jumped up and disappeared into the back of the restaurant. She returned carrying a canvas bag and four torches. She dumped them on the table. There were a few glow knives in the bag, and several soul-catchers. They all took one of each.

'Are you ready?' Oran asked. The others nodded. 'Good. Then let's go.'

13

Andrew, Poppy, Dan, Jason and Oran ventured out into the street. Their torches provided a weak sliver of light in the otherwise pitch-black city. Andrew shone his torch at some long objects in the road. He wasn't sure what they were at first, but when he got closer he realised that they were bodies.

He gulped, and looked ahead, trying not to think about it. 'Where now?' he asked.

'Keep going,' Oran said. 'And don't stop for anyone.'

'I won't,' Andrew said, but just as the words had left his mouth, a girl came running out of the shadows. She was about sixteen, with a beautiful face and long blonde hair, but her ice-blue eyes were wide with fear.

'Help me,' she said. 'I've lost my family. I'm scared. I don't know what to do.'

Poppy bit her lip. 'Don't, Andrew. I think she's—'

'We have to help her,' Andrew said. 'Can't you see that she's scared out of her brain?' He reached out to take the girl's hand. 'It's OK, we're not going to hurt you.' He wanted to comfort her somehow. Not just because she was gorgeous, but also because she seemed so clueless and afraid.

The girl smiled warmly. Despite everything that was going on, Andrew felt his stomach fill with butterflies.

'Andrew,' Poppy said again, this time with more urgency. But Andrew wasn't listening. As he stared into the girl's wide, Bambi-like eyes, he was filled with an unfamiliar yearning. Despite everything that was going on, he couldn't help thinking how beautiful she was…how perfect her rosy cheeks were, and the small dimples at the sides of her mouth, and the sweet perfume she was wearing.

In a daze, he leaned forwards to kiss her.

'Andrew!' Poppy shouted.

The girl's jaw widened into an impossibly large pit. Her perfect teeth grew into sharp spikes, as long as knitting needles. She lunged forwards with her gaping mouth.

Andrew screamed and jerked back to life. He lifted his hands up and sent a pulse of telekinetic energy at the girl, catapulting her into the building behind. She hit the wall with a dull thud and slid slowly to the ground, where she burst into a ball of bright green flames.

'What...the...hell was that thing?' Andrew panted, trying to get his breath back.

'Some kind of siren, I think,' Poppy said. 'Stunning creatures that lure men with their irresistible but false beauty. Dan got tricked by one the other day – nearly lost an arm.' She stifled a laugh. 'Honestly, men! They'll fall for anything as long as it's got a pretty face.'

'Never again,' Andrew said, shaking his head. 'I'm not going near another girl for the rest of my life.'

'I did warn you not to stop for anyone.' Oran smiled.

'Yeah, yeah.' Andrew rolled his eyes. 'Come on.' He started walking again.

'Watch out!' Dan shrieked, yanking him backwards. A group of Shadowmares floated around the corner into the street.

'Get back here,' Dan said. They hurried into the doorway of a shop and crouched down out of view. Andrew gripped the glow knife tightly in his hand, taking deep breaths as the Shadowmares drifted ever closer.

Oran stood a few feet in front of them, holding his unicorn horn up. 'Keep quiet and they should pass,' he whispered. 'But just in case...'

The air grew colder as the Shadowmares floated

towards them. Their black cloaks, made entirely of shadows, trailed behind them like a veil of smoke.

Andrew held his breath as they passed, their burning red eyes fixed straight ahead. He watched as they neared the end of the road, and then wiped the sweat from his brow. *That was close.*

He stumbled back into the street. The air was so bitterly cold he could see his own breath. After a while the road signs indicated that they were in Piccadilly Circus, but Andrew barely recognised the place. Entire buildings were on fire. Angry flames rose high into the sky like giant orange hands, and yet there were no firemen in sight.

'You OK?' Poppy said, putting a hand on his shoulder.

'I'm fine,' Andrew said. And he really was. Six months ago he would have been overcome with fear, but now there were bigger things to worry about.

'Look at that,' Jason said, pointing to a fountain with a statue of an angel.

'So?' Dan said. 'That's always been there, man.'

'Not like that, it hasn't,' Andrew said, his stomach churning. The water was as red as blood, just like Hyde Park's lake had been, trickling down the fountain and onto the pavement like a gushing wound. It poured onto the street, staining the pavement a sickly scarlet.

Andrew looked up. High up on the buildings were massive screens. Usually they had advertisements showing on them, but today, they were playing horror films.

'Wow,' Andrew said, suddenly forgetting everything else. He'd never seen any of these horror films before – they were completely new. He stood mesmerised, watching one of the screens as a man transformed into a hideous werewolf.

'Cooool,' he whispered.

'Andrew!' Poppy screamed, pulling him backwards. 'Watch out.' She yanked him by the collar of his T-shirt. There was a shattering of glass and the werewolf jumped out of the TV screen, leaping towards him. He dived out of the way just in time, then jumped to his feet.

The werewolf prowled towards Andrew, its red eyes fixed on his. Its grey fur was thick and unruly, and its fangs were sharp and stained with blood.

Andrew gulped and lifted his hands in the air. His fingers buzzed and pulsated as if an electric current was soaring through them. Blistering green light exploded out of his palms, hitting the beast square in the chest.

The werewolf paused for a moment, and then continued skulking towards him.

'Why isn't it working?' Andrew shouted, as he sent another pulse of green light at the creature. But it wasn't having any effect. The werewolf arched its back and then leapt at Andrew, pushing him backwards onto the ground. Andrew stared up at the beast, its jaw snapping inches away from his face.

'What do I do? I can't get it off me!'

There was another howl. Andrew turned his head. Five more werewolves had appeared. They stood in a pack, salivating, waiting for their master's signal to jump in for the kill.

13

The pack leader bared its fangs and let out a fierce, ear-piercing growl and the wolves rushed in to begin their feeding frenzy. Andrew felt sharp teeth biting into his left arm. The pain was so intense it was like a hundred screws being forced into his flesh all at once. If he didn't act soon, the werewolves were going to tear him to shreds.

Then, just as the pack leader moved in for Andrew's head, the wolf was tugged backwards, as if it was attached to an invisible string.

Jason was holding the werewolf by the scruff of its neck as it twisted and whined like an injured dog. He tossed it aside, so that it rolled several times on the pavement. There was a huge wound on its back where Jason had injured it with a glow knife. The werewolf crawled back onto all fours again, leaving a few drops of blood on the ground. It hesitated, as if deciding whether to go in for another attack.

'Take another step and your friends get it too,' Jason growled, holding his glow knife in the air.

Oran, Dan and Jason raced over and tried to wrestle the remaining werewolves off Andrew. There was a deafening howl from the pack leader, and the werewolves scurried away into the night.

'Thanks, Jason,' Andrew said, getting to his feet. 'I owe you one.'

'Are you OK?' Poppy asked, rushing over to him. Bone and muscle were poking through his shredded skin. 'OK, stupid question.'

'Why don't you just heal yourself again?' Jason asked.

'No.' Oran shook his head. 'Wounds of this magnitude require a lot of energy to heal. Energy that Andrew will need if we are going to rescue everyone from the Fear Farms. I'll use my unicorn horn instead.'

'But what about you?' Andrew said. He knew that Oran's unicorn horn only contained a limited amount of power. Once used up, it took time to restore the magic again. But Oran had already begun moving his unicorn horn over Andrew's body, from his feet upwards. It gave off a neon purple glow, so bright that Andrew had to shield his eyes. A deep itch ran all the way up his body, like a million ants were crawling under his skin. He clenched his fists, resisting the urge to scratch.

'Wow,' Jason said, grinning. 'That's amazing! You're almost healed.'

'Is it nearly over?' Andrew asked, gritting his teeth.

'Yes, it's over.' Oran smiled, lowering the unicorn horn, which was now only emitting a faint glow. 'How are you feeling?'

'Better than ever,' Andrew smiled.

'Good. Now, there are three entrances into Piccadilly tube station, and I suspect that Vesuvius will have the Shadowmares guarding all three. They probably have instructions to kill anyone who enters, except Andrew, of course. They'll want him alive.'

'So what do we do?' Andrew said, not taking his eyes off the big screens even for a second, scared that more creatures might come diving out of them again.

'Andrew and Jason, you can take the main entrance. I'll take the second, and Poppy and Dan can take the third. That way, we'll have each of them covered and we'll sneak up on them. You know the score. Use the glow knives as soon as you see any Shadowmares. Once they're injured, trap them inside the soul-catchers.'

'Right, man,' Dan said. 'Let's do this.'

'Good luck,' Poppy said, as they crossed the road towards the second entrance.

'You too,' Andrew said. He didn't like the thought of being separated from his twin, even for just a moment, but he knew that she'd be safe with Dan.

He hurried with Jason to the nearest entrance. The metal signs along the top usually read 'Public Subway' and 'Underground' but they'd been painted over with something new.

'Fear Farm Number 005,' Andrew read aloud.

'Creepy, isn't it?' Jason said. 'They've done that to all the tube stations.'

Andrew sighed. 'I wonder how many people are trapped down there. Hundreds, I bet.'

'Possibly more,' Jason said with a grim expression. 'They've built Fear Farms all over the country, maybe even the world, in any underground place they can find.'

Another pang of guilt. And it was all because of *his* fear. 'Come on,' Andrew said, marching ahead. 'Let's go and kill some Shadowmares.'

They crept down the steps to the tube station. Andrew felt a burst of cold air and the hairs shot up on his arms. *The Shadowmares were close.* He slowed his pace and hugged the wall. Jason crept quietly behind him.

'There,' Andrew whispered, pointing at three

Shadowmares guarding the point where the steps ended. 'I'll take the middle Shadowmare and the one on the right. You can deal with the other one. Cool?'

'Sounds fair to me,' Jason said.

'We run at them on three. Got it?'

Jason nodded.

'OK: one, two…' Andrew paused, taking a deep breath. 'Three.'

They charged at the Shadowmares. The adrenaline was pumping through his veins like he'd just downed a litre of coffee. He clenched the glow knife tightly in his hand, and then pressed it hard into the Shadowmare standing in the middle, catching it off guard. It groaned as it collapsed to the ground, its red eyes flickering like the dying flame of a candle. Andrew pulled the blade out and spun to his right. A rush of cold air hit him like a truck. The other Shadowmare was blowing icy breath over Andrew. For a moment, every muscle in his body tensed up. Gritting his teeth, he tried to fight the cold. He moved stiffly towards the Shadowmare. With all his might, he brought the glow knife down onto the creature's shoulder. There was a loud shattering of bones, and the Shadowmare slumped to the ground. Andrew pulled out the soul-catcher from his bag and turned to face Jason, who was leaning against the wall, breathless. There were two Shadowmares on the ground.

'Where did the third one go?' Andrew asked.

'It disappeared into thin air,' Jason said. 'I stabbed it with the glow knife, and then the next second, poof, it was gone.'

Andrew nodded.

'Yeah, sometimes that happens. If you don't injure them badly enough, they transport themselves back to the Nightmare Factory. Sucks that we didn't kill it, but at least it's out of our way.' Footsteps echoed towards them. Andrew glanced up, searching the tube station. Poppy and Dan were strolling towards them.

'All done, man,' Dan said, patting his soul-catcher, which now contained swirling black smoke. 'These bad boys ain't coming back.'

Andrew paused. 'Where's Oran?'

'I'm here.' Oran staggered towards them, one hand pressed to a cut above his eyebrow, which was gushing blood.

'Oran!' Andrew said, running up to him. 'What happened?'

'Oh, I'm fine. It looks worse than it is. Shall we get moving?'

The tube station looked completely different to how Andrew remembered it. There were only a few lights working, so it was cast in flickering shadows. The ticket machines had all been ripped up from the ground and in their place was a long metal gate.

Andrew frowned. It seemed too easy. He walked up to the gate and tried to open it. A sharp pain travelled all the way up to his shoulder and he was thrown backwards onto the floor.

'Ouch!' He shook his hand. 'That really hurt.'

'What is it?' Jason asked. He crept up to the gate.

'Are you alright, dude?' Dan said. 'You must be in shock. Ha ha! Get it? In shock!'

'Hilarious,' Andrew growled.

'Do you think it's magically protected?' Poppy said, keeping her distance.

'No.' Andrew shook his head. 'I think it's just a normal electric fence. There must be a switch around here somewhere. Maybe we can find a way to turn it off.' He shone his torch around the walls.

'There,' Jason shouted, pointing to a plug. 'Try that.'

Andrew hurried over to it and yanked the plug out of the socket. 'OK, who's going to be our canary, then? I would, but if I get zapped again, I think it might finish me off. And Oran's already hurt.'

'No way, man,' Dan said, folding his arms. 'I'm not going anywhere near that thing.'

Andrew rolled his eyes.

'I'll do it,' Jason said, stepping towards the gate.

'See,' Andrew said. 'At least someone's got guts around here.'

Dan scowled, and mumbled something under his breath as Jason reached gingerly out to touch the gate.

Nothing happened. Jason smiled. 'It's off,' he said, looking relieved. He opened the gate up wide, and crept over to the escalators. Andrew followed, gasping loudly when he reached the top. The underground station was full of hundreds of Fear Pods, lodged tightly together like a stack of Jenga bricks. Thick wires coiled out from each pod and disappeared into the walls on either side.

'This is terrible,' Poppy said. 'There are so many of them.'

There was a person inside every pod, although from this distance, Andrew couldn't make out if any of them were Tiffany or his mum.

'How did they build all of these so quickly?' he said.

'Vesuvius had people working on them day and night like slaves,' Dan whispered. 'Come on, let's start setting them free.'

They hurtled down the escalator, jumping every other step as they went.

'How long do you think we have before the rest of the Shadowmares come back?' Andrew asked.

'A while,' Jason said. 'We've spent a few nights watching them. They usually start returning around seven, just before the sun comes up.'

Andrew glanced at his watch. 12.06 am. They had plenty of time.

'There may be a few Shadowmares still guarding the area, so keep your eyes peeled,' Oran warned them.

There were metal ladders leading up to all of the pods.

'Right, get moving,' Oran said, climbing up one of them. Andrew put a foot on one of the ladders and heaved himself up to the nearest pod. Inside was an old man. He was wearing a dressing gown and slippers and was tied down to the seat inside the pod.

'Help me, boy. Please help me. I have a wife and grandkids at home.'

'I will,' Andrew told him, as he took off his jumper. 'Shut your eyes,' he said.

The man frowned, but then screwed his eyes shut. Andrew wrapped the jumper around his fist and took a swing at the glass pod, shattering it completely.

He could hear glass exploding all around him as the others hurried around, doing the same thing. He wondered if Poppy had found their mum or Tiffany yet.

An icy breeze filled the room. It was so sudden, Andrew nearly passed out from the cold. He spun around. The Shadowmares were flooding down the escalators like an army of ants, scrambling over one another to get to the pods. There were thousands of them, more than Andrew had ever laid eyes on before. How did they know that they were here? Had they been followed?

'Andrew!' he heard Poppy call. She sounded close by.

'Climb down the ladders,' Andrew yelled. 'We need to get out of here.'

'No,' the old man said. 'Please. Don't leave me here to die. Get me out of here.'

'We'll come back for you,' Andrew said, and he clambered down the nearest ladder. Jason followed him, and Dan, Poppy and Oran appeared from around the other side.

'We're trapped,' Dan said, staring up at the Shadowmares swarming in from above.

'Quick, Jason, the map. Where is the nearest exit?'

Jason fumbled with the map, hands trembling. 'Through there,' he said, pointing to one of the walkways. 'We can travel north-east along the train tracks, and we'll end up at Leicester Square.'

'Right, let's go,' Andrew said, setting off at a run. They came to a flight of stairs and hurried down them.

There were tracks on either side. Poppy turned to head right.

'No, this way,' Jason said, tugging at her sleeve. 'We need to go left.'

They followed Jason down the platform and jumped down onto the tracks. It was a steep drop, and Andrew felt his knees jar as his feet hit the ground. They raced into the dark tunnel. The coldness was unbearable, seeping deep into his veins. Andrew looked back. The Shadowmares were quickly gaining on them.

Andrew was running as fast as he could, but his feet were growing more rigid with every step. Poppy, Dan and Oran were keeping pace beside him, groaning with exhaustion. Jason was struggling far behind. He stopped, catching his breath.

'What are you doing? Get a move on,' Dan called back to him. 'They're going to catch you.'

'I've got a stitch!' Jason yelled.

Andrew stopped dead. There was a wall of bars reaching from the top of the tunnel to the floor, blocking their exit. He put his hands up against them. Hopelessness swelled inside him. 'We can't go any further.'

'What do you mean, man?' Dan said, catching up.

Andrew turned. There was an unending sea of blackness hurtling towards them at full speed. Another set of bars crashed down before him, trapping them in some sort of cage. It was as if they had appeared from nowhere. Jason was standing outside the bars, Shadowmares ploughing towards him.

'Jason,' Andrew screamed. 'Can you get us out of here?'

Jason smiled. 'Dunno. Why should I?'

'What do you mean? We've got an army of Shadowmares coming up. We need to—' He stopped talking. Vesuvius had appeared beside Jason, as if he had been waiting in the shadows all along.

'You did well, Jason,' Vesuvius smiled, patting him on the back.

15

Jason grinned.

Buds of sickness spawned inside of Andrew. 'Jason, what does he mean by that?'

'Please tell me you didn't help him,' Poppy said, her voice cracking.

Jason nodded, puffing out his chest. He seemed to grow a little taller. He strolled up to the bars, looking Andrew straight in the eyes. 'I had you fooled all along. Right from the very beginning, didn't I?'

'Huh?' Andrew said. He couldn't believe it. He didn't *want* to believe it.

'I've done what you asked of me now, Vesuvius. Can I have my reward?'

What reward? thought Andrew. What had he done this for? *Money? Freedom… Respect?*

Vesuvius turned to Jason. His eyes narrowed. 'I still have use for you.' He clicked his bony fingers. There was a sharp snapping sound, and the next thing Andrew saw was Oran's unicorn horn flying out of his hands and into Vesuvius's.

'Here,' he said, handing it to Jason. 'Guard them for me.'

Jason's eyes widened in amazement as he reached out and took the glowing unicorn horn.

'Be careful not to kill the boy,' Vesuvius hissed. 'I have a Fear Pod being built for him. You can do what you like with the others.' He turned and headed back down the tunnel.

'Jason,' Andrew said, pressing his face up against the bars. 'This is ludicrous. Why are you doing this?'

'Why?' Jason said, storming up to the cage. 'I'll tell you *why*.' His dark eyes were sparkling with malice. He sounded like a crazy person.

He's actually enjoying this... Andrew thought, feeling sick.

'You think you're so much better than everyone else. All high-and-mighty and courageous, prancing around trying to save the world with your *powers*.' He spat out the last word with such mockery and hatred that Andrew wondered if he really was crazy. 'Look at you now. You're nothing.' He pointed the unicorn horn at Andrew's feet and fired green light at him. 'Dance for me, Andrew, dance!' Andrew jumped out of the way, and Jason laughed.

'I don't know what you're talking about,' Andrew said, dodging another flare of light. 'I don't think I'm better than anyone.'

Jason stopped. His face turned serious again.

'At the market, you made everyone laugh at me.'

'What? When? That's stupid. I don't know what you're on abou—' The words caught in his throat as his mind reeled back to several months ago, when he'd pushed a bully across the street for stealing Poppy's money. It was the first time he'd used his powers. He stared at Jason. It couldn't be...*could it?*

'Remember now?' Jason asked, a wicked glint in his eyes.

Dan came and stood beside him. 'Andrew, what's he talking about, man?'

Andrew didn't answer. How had he not realised?

'But you can't be the boy that Andrew pushed,' Poppy said. 'He had blond hair and he was built like a ton of bricks.'

'Never heard of contacts or hair dye?' Jason smirked. 'I lost some weight. Hoped you wouldn't recognise me. I outsmarted you.' He laughed again.

'Jason,' Andrew said, firmly. 'This is getting out of hand. You've got to let us out of here. Whatever problems you have with me, you need to put them aside. Don't you realise that Vesuvius is going to destroy the whole world with my fear? Now he's got what he wants, he won't care what happens to you.'

Jason's eyes narrowed. He stepped forwards, so that it was only the bars between them.

'See, that's where you're wrong, Andrew. We have a deal. He respects me.'

'Vesuvius respects no one,' Oran said. It was the first time he'd spoken since Vesuvius had taken his unicorn horn and given it to Jason. He was sitting in the corner of the cell, holding his bleeding head.

'Shut up, old man,' Jason hissed. 'I didn't ask you.' He pointed the unicorn horn at Oran and sent a green blaze of light shooting into his chest. Oran clutched his heart, falling onto his side.

Jason laughed.

'That's out of order, man!' Dan screamed, rushing forwards. Poppy grabbed his arm, holding him back. Andrew was fuming. There was no way he was going to let Jason get away with hurting Oran. He sent a burst of telekinetic energy at him, throwing him against the tunnel wall.

'Don't ever hurt my friends like that again!' Andrew screamed.

For a few seconds, Jason just lay there. *Have I killed him?* Andrew wondered, but then Jason got slowly to his feet, rubbing his back. Andrew raised his hands again, expecting Jason to fight back, but he stood with his fists curled into two tight balls, face crimson with rage. 'You're going to regret doing that,' he said, glaring at Andrew. He picked up the unicorn horn and stormed off up the tunnel.

'He's gone,' Oran said. 'This is your chance.'

'This is *our* chance,' Andrew corrected him. 'I'm going to get us out of here and you're coming with us.' He focused all of his energy on the bars. The pressure filled his head like a balloon being pumped full of air. Sweat poured from his brow. Slowly, the gap between two bars widened as Andrew bent them outwards with all the force of his mind.

'That's it, that's the widest I can get them to bend,' Andrew said, letting out all of his breath at once. He slumped to the ground, exhausted.

'I'll never be able to fit through a gap the size of that,' Oran said, shaking his head. 'But it's OK, Andrew; you go without me.'

Poppy walked over to Oran and sat next to him. 'We're not leaving you.'

'She's right,' Dan said. 'We're in this together.'

'Then we'll all die,' Oran said. 'Us and the rest of the world.'

'OK,' Andrew said. 'I see what you're doing. But you don't get it. If we leave you here, Oran, Vesuvius will *kill* you.'

'Yeah,' Poppy said. 'And that's if Jason doesn't first.'

'Perhaps,' Oran said. 'But I'm willing to take my chances. I beg you, Andrew, go.'

Andrew bit his lip, holding back tears. He knew that Oran was talking sense, but he couldn't bring himself to admit it. 'Let me have another go at bending the bars.'

'No,' Oran said, slamming his hand down against the floor. 'Go now. While you still have the chance.'

Poppy stood up. 'Come on, Andrew,' she said, taking his hand. 'Oran's right.'

Andrew shook his head, wiping back tears. He threw his arms around Oran.

'I swear, if either Vesuvius or that creep Jason touch you, I'll kill them. I'll—' He stopped, choking back tears.

Oran smiled. 'I'll be fine, Andrew. Now go.' He ushered Andrew out of the space between the bars.

Andrew turned sideways and squeezed through the narrow gap. Poppy followed closely behind him, and then Dan.

'Wait. How are we supposed to get everyone out of the Fear Farms now? We're two people down.'

'Sometimes plans require deviations,' Oran said, bowing his head. 'Go to Nusquam. Tarker will inform you of the rest.'

'Huh? Why Nusquam?' Andrew said. 'And how do we get there?'

'Go to the same portal that we arrived at,' Oran said quickly. 'You remember what to do, don't you?'

Andrew nodded.

'Good. Now leave and don't turn back.'

The temperature in the tunnel dropped. Oran spun around. The Shadowmares were floating towards them in their hundreds, like an army marching into war. Jason was striding ahead, holding Oran's unicorn horn high in the air.

'We'll come back for you, Oran,' Andrew said, and he turned, sprinting into the darkness of the tunnel.

A deafening symphony of screams chilled the air. For a moment Andrew froze, terror sweeping through him.

Oran.

'Come on,' Poppy said, grabbing his hand. 'You can't save him now.' She dragged him, forcing him to run faster and faster into the blackness of the tunnel.

Tears stung at his face as the screams got louder, echoing against the stone walls. And he knew, deep down, that he'd never see his friend again.

16

A small circle of light drifted into view, growing bigger and bigger as they ran closer towards it. Nobody said a word until they reached the end of the tunnel. Andrew felt numb, replaying Oran's screams over and over again in his head like a broken record. Guilt gnawed away at him. *Could they have saved him, if only they'd turned back?*

'Stop it,' Poppy said.

'Stop what?'

'Stop blaming yourself for what happened. It's not your fault.'

Andrew hauled himself up onto Leicester Square platform. He just wanted to get out of this horrible place.

'The Shadowmares will be expecting us,' Poppy said. 'Get back down here. We need to carry on down the tunnel and exit at Covent Garden.'

'How can you act so normal?'

Poppy looked up. 'What do you mean?'

'Like that didn't just happen? Like we didn't just

walk away and leave Oran to die?' He choked, trying not to cry. 'It's as if you're not even upset by it.'

'Not upset?' Poppy said, tears beading in her eyes. Her fists were clenched by her sides. 'I loved Oran. I'm just trying to make sure that you get out of here alive. I'm trying to make sure that he didn't die for nothing.'

Andrew fell silent. He didn't have anything to say to that.

'Look, she's right. Can we just get out of here?' Dan said, grim-faced.

They were all on tenterhooks.

'OK,' Andrew said bluntly, lowering himself back down onto the tracks. He didn't feel like speaking. He was numb with shock, anger, sadness…but most of all, guilt. He'd trusted Jason. He'd trusted him with their lives, and Oran had been the one to pay the price.

They jogged the rest of the way, too exhausted to sprint and too weighed down by grief to care. Andrew turned his head. There was no sign of the Shadowmares, but the darkness of the tunnel was unrelenting. He couldn't even see his feet moving one in front of the other as he ran deeper into the tunnel

After ten minutes, light began to filter back through again.

'Finally,' Dan said, gasping for breath.

The electric lights were blinding. They hoisted themselves up onto the Covent Garden platform and crept along the wall, careful to be as quiet as possible.

'Keep your glow knives handy,' Andrew whispered. 'We might not need them, but chances are there'll be a few Shadowmares guarding the exits.'

Poppy and Dan nodded, and reached into their backpacks. They climbed the steps and tiptoed along the walkway into the main part of the tube station. A lot of the walls had been knocked down to make extra space for Fear Pods. Andrew counted them with his eyes. There were about a hundred in total, packed together like battery chickens' cages. What if their mum was in one of them? Or Tiffany Grey? He desperately wanted to go and set them all free. *No, stupid idea.* Their main priority now was getting to Nusquam. He owed Oran that much at least.

Andrew looked away, trying to ignore the hundreds of desperate pleading faces.

'I'll come back for you,' he whispered. *Another broken promise?* He took a deep breath, trying to bury the feeling of utter hopelessness and sorrow that had nested inside of him, multiplying like some sort of deadly virus.

He had to ignore it. Had to be strong.

They tumbled onto the escalator.

'Get down,' Poppy whispered. She pulled on Andrew's arm. 'We need to stay as inconspicuous as possible, remember?'

'You're right,' Andrew said, crouching. They climbed slowly upwards. When they reached the top, Andrew stayed ducked whilst he tiptoed over to the gate. It was as large and as tall as the one in Piccadilly Circus.

'I'll go and disable the electricity,' Dan whispered. He crept over to the wall in search of the plug. He pulled it out, and gave Andrew the thumbs up.

'Right,' Andrew said. 'We need to reach the nearest exit without disturbing any of the Shadowmares. We might be able to kill two or three, but any more and we'll have a problem.'

Poppy nodded, and pushed open the gate. Andrew held his breath, praying that it wouldn't squeak. Luckily, it glided open.

They turned down an exit. Two Shadowmares stood facing the street. Andrew lifted his glow knife, signalling for Dan to do the same with his. Poppy stood behind them, holding the soul-catcher ready.

'Hey,' Andrew said, tapping the left Shadowmare on the back.

Both creatures spun around with flaming red eyes.

He twisted the glow knife into their stomachs, before the cold numbing effect could reach his arms. Dan did the same with his. The shimmering blue blades pierced through their flesh and bones, lighting them up from the insides like Chinese lanterns. The Shadowmares groaned and hissed, falling to the ground.

'Now!' Andrew shouted, and Poppy rushed out from behind the gate, holding the soul-catcher high in the air. The Shadowmares' smoky black cloaks twisted and coiled until they were finally sucked into the glass flasks. Andrew stepped over the two skeletons lying on the pavement.

'That's for Oran,' Andrew said.

They raced up the steps and out into the cool breeze.

Panic ran high on the streets of London. Children and adults were fleeing in every direction. A group of headless horsemen cantered past, brandishing swords. Andrew quickly ducked as one of them took a swipe at his neck.

'Over there!' Dan screamed.

Across the road, some sort of beast, like a giant yeti, stumbled towards them. They picked up speed. The pavement began to rumble. Then, like a carpet pulled from under their feet, it lifted up as if it was breathing, throwing Andrew, Poppy and Dan onto the road.

'It's as if it's alive,' Andrew said, rolling onto his back. 'As if the city is trying to kill us.'

'Maybe it is,' Dan said dryly. 'Nothing makes sense any more.'

'We're never going to get to the portal at this rate,' Poppy said, getting back up. 'We need a plan, and fast.'

Dan looked around the ruined street, thick with smoke and dust as if a bomb had gone off. His eyes paused over an abandoned car.

Andrew laughed. 'You can't be serious?'

'Perfectly,' Dan said. His face was firm. He didn't flinch.

Andrew sighed. 'How many reasons do you want me to give you why that is a really bad idea?'

Dan shrugged. 'How many have you got?'

'OK, for starters you're fifteen,' Poppy said, before Andrew had the chance. 'You don't even know how to drive a car.'

'I know where the brake pedal and the accelerator are. How hard can it be?'

There came a thunderous groan from behind them. Andrew spun around. A group of creatures stood

157

staring hungrily at them with skin sewn together like a patchwork doll. Blood dripped from every seam. And their teeth; Andrew couldn't take his eyes off their teeth. A giant set of spikes so sharp and pointed, they looked as if they could chew straight through bone.

'OK,' Andrew said, trying to gather his thoughts. 'Quick!' he shouted, grabbing Poppy's arm and dragging her towards the car. The front doors were sprawled open like wings, as if someone had made a quick escape. The keys were still in the ignition. Dan jumped into the driver's seat and Poppy tumbled into the back. Andrew took the passenger seat and slammed the door, just as the patchwork creatures smacked up against the glass.

'Drive,' he said, tugging on his seatbelt. 'Now.'

For a few moments, Dan stared blankly at the controls.

'What are you doing?' Poppy shouted from the back. 'Get going!'

'I-I don't know what to do.'

Andrew turned to him. 'What? I thought you said it would be easy?'

'Well, I assumed it would be an automatic.'

There was a loud thud as one of the patchwork

creatures climbed onto the bonnet of the car. It took a swing at the windscreen and a small crack appeared in the glass.

'We don't have a lot of time,' Andrew said, looking out of the side window as a jumble of veiny hands hammered against it. 'This glass isn't going to hold forever. Switch with me. I'll have to drive.'

'What?' Dan said. 'Do you even know how?'

'No,' Andrew said honestly. 'But I reckon I could at least get it started.'

They switched places. Andrew turned the keys. There was a groan as the engine fired and then died. The car lurched forwards, throwing the patchwork creature into the road, and then jerked to a standstill.

'So much for getting it started,' Dan muttered.

'You stalled. I think you gotta work the clutch,' Poppy said.

'Yeah, I know,' Andrew hissed, irritated. He tried the ignition again. There was a roar from the engine and the car shot into the road. He yanked the steering wheel right, narrowly missing a building. 'This driving business is trickier than it looks,' he said. He pushed his foot down on the clutch, putting the car into second gear. It grumbled as if it was about to stall again, but he managed to save it just in time. Andrew checked the speed dial. Thirty miles per hour. The car was chugging like it had swallowed a can of sewage.

Andrew had some idea of how gears worked from watching his mum drive. He stuck it into third and the car glided smoothly. He smiled. He was getting the hang of this!

He drove through a set of red lights. There were no other cars on the road, so he figured it was no big deal.

'Careful, man,' Dan said as they careered towards two people. Andrew swerved to avoid them. The car shot up onto the kerb instead, ploughing into a shop.

Andrew was thrown forwards. His nose smacked against the steering wheel. He could feel the warm trickle of blood pouring out of it.

'Everyone OK?' he said, cupping the flow of blood with his hands.

'Uh-huh,' Dan said, groaning from the passenger seat.

'Yep,' Poppy croaked. 'I'm alive. Just about.'

'Good. It's not far from here. We can probably run the rest of the way.'

Andrew swung the door open and leapt out, leaving the keys in the ignition in case the car's owner came back at any point. Although he doubted that they would.

They sprinted down the road, running past a group of clowns with white faces and curly orange hair. They had brooches pinned to their outfits in the shape of flowers, which they were squirting at everything in sight. Andrew dodged a spray of water.

'Wow, close one,' Poppy said, as it hit the wall behind them.

'What?' Andrew turned, and saw that the water had not been water at all, but some kind of acid. It burned the wall away, chewing through the concrete as if it was paper.

'Oh no, I hate clowns,' Dan said, picking up speed.

They reached a giant, hairy spider, taller than most of the buildings. Poppy froze, turning pale.

'Under its legs,' Andrew said. 'Quick, before it notices us!' He grabbed her by the arm and dragged her forward, as they wove in and out of the tarantula's big, hairy limbs. Andrew laughed despite himself. It looked like a scene from a movie. He half expected someone to jump out at any moment with a clipboard and shout, 'Cut!'

But that wasn't going to happen. Because this was *real*. He snapped out of the fantasy and concentrated on running. They reached the entrance of Hyde Park.

'Don't get too close to the lake,' Andrew said,

remembering the strange lake monster with huge tentacles. Poppy was staring at him inquisitively. 'Don't ask,' he said, shaking his head.

They ran up the grassy hill. They were almost at the bench, when there was a scream from behind. Andrew spun around. Dan was being pulled into a patch of mud, as if it was quicksand. He clawed at the grass, trying to stop himself from sinking any further. Andrew dived forwards.

'Quick! Take my hand. I'll pull you out.'

He grabbed Dan's hand. The mud was as thick as treacle and at first Dan wouldn't budge. Then he shot free like a cork from a bottle. They flew backwards and landed on a patch of grass behind them.

Andrew jumped to his feet. 'Hurry, before it sucks us under again.'

The bench was in sight. They raced over to it, panting hard. Andrew collapsed onto the wooden seat, exhaustion getting the better of him. Every joint and muscle in his body was twitching and throbbing. Tears stained his face. He thought of Oran, and all he wanted to do was curl up into a tiny ball and go to sleep. He shut his eyes, only for a second, relishing the silence.

The sound of gurgling water pulled him back to

reality. He opened his eyes to see a green tentacle erupting from the blood-red lake. It swung towards them, rimmed with a million sharp teeth.

'Get down!' Andrew yelled, shoving Dan and Poppy out of the way.

The creature's tentacle glided over their heads, missing them by mere centimetres. Then it disappeared underwater again.

'Yowzers! What was that thing?' Dan said, staring at the bubbling lake.

Andrew shrugged. 'Not sure.'

'Well, thanks anyway, man. Hey, do you think we could get out of here now?'

'Good idea,' Andrew said. 'Shut your eyes and think of Oran's Dream Factory. I'll worry about the rest.' He tried to remember the rhyme. 'Aska Babaka, Nusquam arrow. Take us to where we want to go!'

Andrew opened one eye. He was still sitting on the park bench. His stomach dropped. *It hadn't worked. Had he forgotten something?*

A bright flash of light exploded around them. Andrew felt himself spinning over and over, doing somersaults through the air. He was thrown into a tunnel of space and light, soaring through it at an immense speed. Somewhere from behind him, he could hear Poppy and Dan's faint screams.

He landed with a thud on Oran's dining room floor. He sat up, head still spinning. How had Oran managed to land with such grace earlier?

He swallowed, blinking back tears. He couldn't believe he was no longer alive.

A seam of light appeared above the rug, as if the air had been ripped in two. From within the crack, Poppy and Dan came hurtling out, rolling onto the floor in a tangled mess of limbs.

'*Urgh!*' Dan grunted, sitting up. His face was a pale shade of green. 'That was way worse than I expected. I think I'm going to puke.' His cheeks bulged and he rushed over to the bin. There was an awful retching sound as he was sick.

'Me too,' Poppy said, holding her stomach.

Someone coughed loudly from over by the door. Andrew spun around, and spotted Tarker standing there, cradling a tiny baby with translucent blue skin.

Tarker was one of Oran's many workers at the Dream Factory. The Luguarna people had an odd appearance. The males, like Tarker, had bald heads and very pink skin. And the females had bright blue skin. All of them were short, no bigger than a four-year-old child.

'Hello, Andrew,' Tarker said, smiling. 'Dan, Poppy.' He nodded his head. 'Where's Oran?'

'Tarker,' Dan said quietly. 'Listen, man, there's something you need to know.'

Tarker's face turned grave. 'Oran's dead, isn't he?'

A lump grew in Andrew's throat. 'Yes,' he croaked. 'But how did you know?'

Tarker sighed. 'Just a feeling, I suppose.' He turned to leave, and then stopped. 'Follow me. I have something to give you.'

Andrew wiped a tear from his eyes. 'What is it?'

Tarker shrugged and pointed to the door. Luguarna people never were ones for speaking much.

They followed Tarker through the brightly-lit corridor. Andrew had been here before, but the grandeur of the place still amazed him. Many of the windows were stained glass, but they still allowed the light to flood through from outside in glittering purple rays.

They arrived at a room marked 'Oran's Office'. Tarker took a ring of keys from his pocket and unlocked the door. Inside was a glass desk covered in papers and piled high with books. A silver chair, shaped like an egg, sat behind it.

'Why have you brought us here?' Andrew asked.

Silence. Ripples of light filtered through a blind behind the desk. Tarker hobbled over to it and drew it shut, then turned back around. He stood on his tiptoes to reach a drawer, and pulled out a small metal box that he placed on top of the desk. He slotted a key inside and the lid clicked open. He pulled out a small silver object, which looked like a Rubik's cube, and a large brown envelope then handed the envelope to Andrew who began to peel back the rim.

'Don't open it yet. I have something else to show you,' Tarker said. He waddled into the centre of the room and began fiddling with the cube.

'What's he doing?' Poppy whispered.

Dan rolled his eyes. 'What's it look like he's doing, numbnuts? He's trying to solve a puzzle.'

'Yes, I see that. But why?'

'No idea.' Andrew shrugged, watching Tarker as he concentrated on turning the squares.

Tarker placed it on the floor and stepped away. The cube buzzed and vibrated. A strange blue light shone out from every crack. It broke apart piece by piece, and a warm glow shot out, rippling the air like a reflection on water. Andrew blinked as the image came into focus. He gasped. It was an image of Oran.

Andrew stood frozen. 'What is that thing?' he asked.

166

'A holographic message,' Tarker said. 'Listen carefully.'

The image of Oran flickered like the flame of a candle and then slowly became more stable.

'Hello, Andrew, Poppy and Dan,' Oran said, beaming widely. 'If you are watching this, then Vesuvius has taken over the world with his army of Shadowmares and I am already dead. Tiffany is also either dead, or in great danger, so I need you to listen very carefully. Please, do not feel sad for me, as it was my time. You must concentrate on the present, and also on the future. There is only one thing that can be done to stop Vesuvius from completely destroying the world now.' The holographic image of Oran glanced over his shoulder, as if to make sure that nobody was watching.

Andrew stood up straight, finding himself peering over his shoulder as well.

'The Fender's Feather,' Oran said.

'The what?' Dan said, as if he was expecting a reply.

Oran began to chuckle. 'You are probably wondering what that is. Well, I will explain.' He glanced around the room again. 'Close the door. Make sure that nobody is listening apart from the three of you. Not even Tarker.'

Andrew turned around. Tarker raised his eyebrows in surprise. 'Don't take it personally, Tarker – it is not that I do not trust you. It is only to keep you safe,' Oran said, as if anticipating his reaction. Tarker shrugged, and waddled out of the room.

To keep him safe? Safe from what? Andrew thought.

'Good,' Oran said after a long pause. 'Now where was I? Oh yes, the Fender bird. The Fender bird was an ancient Nusquarium bird that lived many years ago. It was beautiful, and legend has it that it used to light up the night sky like a shooting star. But it was slain for its magical feathers. One of these feathers in particular had the capacity to act as a dreamcatcher for the entire world. It has the power to protect every single person from their nightmares. I'll try to be quick, because we don't have much time, but as the story goes, Vesuvius tracked the feather down and tried to destroy it. But no matter what he tried, he failed – it was indestructible. So he did the next best thing. He hid it somewhere that only he could access. Up until a few weeks ago, I believed the entire story to be a myth; otherwise I would have gone after the feather myself. But recent events have led me to believe that it is in fact true. If you can find this feather, and safely bring it back to the Dream Factory, we can rid the world of evil once and for all. But there is a catch.'

Dan groaned. 'Great. I was hoping he wouldn't say that.'

Poppy elbowed him in the side. '*Shh!* Shut up and listen.'

'I believe that Vesuvius has hidden the feather in the Dreamsphere. But he will not have made it easy to find. He will have put many traps in place, all of them deadly. Look in the brown envelope I have left for you,' Oran said. 'You will find the items that you will need to get you started. I apologise for my vagueness, and for not having brought this up with you before, but you must understand that if Vesuvius knew you were planning on going after this feather, he would have killed all of you without a second thought – even you, Andrew. Go to Nusquam Town and find Moonsnake Bill. Tell him I have sent you. Trust Moonsnake and no one else. Now I say goodbye and wish you all the very best of luck. Remember, in the Dreamsphere, things are not always as they seem.'

With that, the holographic image of Oran disappeared, and the light was sucked back into the Rubik's cube again. The little probe that had been projecting the image wound back down and the squares slotted themselves back together again, switching back into their original position. Andrew picked it up. He played with it and shook it, but nothing happened. He placed it back on the desk.

'So, what's in the envelope?' Poppy asked.

Andrew ripped it open as Poppy and Dan crowded around him. He pulled out a map of Nusquam, and then a small glass vial with a label stuck on it.

'Grimble Whatt's dream,' Dan read aloud. 'Who's Grimble Whatt?'

'Who knows? Poppy said. 'More importantly, what's the Dreamsphere?'

'No idea.' Andrew shrugged. 'But I guess we'll find out soon enough.' He put the glass vial back in the envelope and handed the compass to Poppy. 'Let's go,' he said, moving towards the door. 'We have a journey to Nusquam to make.'

17

'Where are you going?' Tarker asked them, trying to keep up as they walked briskly down the corridor towards the dining room.

Dan shook his head. 'You know we can't tell you that, Tarker.'

'Well, can I come with you? I'd like to help.'

'Sorry, Tarker, you have a baby to look after. That's probably why Oran didn't want you getting involved in the first place. He's trying to protect you both. We'll be back soon, and we'll explain everything then.'

Tarker nodded. 'OK,' he said. 'Do you need anything before you go? Anything at all?'

Andrew paused for a moment, thinking. 'Yes. Can we use the Satebite oven?'

Tarker shrugged. 'Sure. If you're hungry I can whip you up some—'

'No, it's fine. We'll do it. Thanks, Tarker.'

Tarker nodded, and then beamed. 'Good luck,' he said, leaving the room.

'I'm starving. What shall we have?' Dan said, picking up the cookbook full of pictures.

'I don't want to make food,' Andrew said, snatching the book off him. 'Do you still have that Nusquarium money that Oran gave you?'

'Err, yes, why?'

'Give it here,' Andrew said, holding out his hand.

Dan reached into his trouser pocket and pulled out the crumpled Nusquarium money. He handed it to Andrew, who placed it under the Satebite oven.

'I'm not sure if this will work or not, but it's worth a try.'

'If what will work?' Dan said, folding his arms. 'You can't eat money.'

'You're trying to replicate the Nusquarium money? I'm pretty sure that's highly illegal.' Poppy said, raising an eyebrow. 'But pretty genius at the same time, I suppose.'

Andrew grinned. 'I figured if we're going to Nusquam Town, then we'll need some cash to take with us. We don't know who we'll have to bribe once we get there.'

He turned the knob on the Satebite oven. At first nothing happened, and then the machine began to buzz like a bee trapped in a jar. A flash of bright light burst out at them, and a second note appeared as if from nowhere.

Andrew punched the air with his first. 'Yes!' he said. 'It actually worked.'

'Now *that* was cool,' Dan said, with a huge grin. 'If we make it back alive, remind me to print some UK money. I could really do with some new Xbox games.'

'Now we just have to make a few more of these,' Poppy said, placing the two notes under the Satebite oven and turning the knob again.

They repeated the process several times, until they had collected a huge wad of cash. Andrew counted the money.

'Seventy sacks,' he said, placing it in a neat pile on the table. 'I have no idea how much that is, of course.'

'It'll be enough,' Poppy said. 'Come on. Let's head outside before it gets too dark.'

'Wait,' Dan said. 'We need to eat before we leave. We don't know how long this journey could take.'

Andrew sighed. He wanted to get going as soon as possible, but Dan was right. And the hunger pains in his stomach agreed.

'OK,' he said. 'Quickly, though.'

Dan took out a picture of a burger and a coke from the book and placed it under the Satebit. After they had finished eating, Andrew shoved the money inside his wallet, and they headed outside into the freezing cold.

Luckily they were already dressed for winter, in thick coats and Wellington boots, but the fierce Nusquarium winds were much harsher than back on Earth. They whipped at their clothes and skin with no remorse. The jagged black mountains towered over the horizon, catching the light like pieces of crystal. They looked beautiful against the violet sky, but Andrew knew otherwise. Nusquam was a dangerous world, where nothing was ever what it seemed.

'I'm starving,' Dan moaned. 'I wish we'd taken some food with us.'

'You only ate half an hour ago,' Poppy said. 'You're hardly going to drop down dead.'

They trudged through the thick covering of snow. It had fallen over everything like a layer of sickening pink Angel Delight, but in many patches it had been blackened with dirt. It continued to fall in chunks, making it almost impossible to see more than a few feet ahead.

'Which way now?' Poppy asked, trying to stop her hair from blowing in her eyes.

Andrew got the map out again, gripping it tightly

so that it wasn't torn away by the wind. It was old-looking, and foxed at the edges, as if someone had dropped it in a pot of tea. Andrew could just make out the faded print.

'Straight ahead according to this,' he said. 'We should come to a statue of Vesuvius soon. That's how we'll know if we're on the right track. We're still going north, right?'

Poppy checked her compass and nodded.

'Good. Then keep on trucking.'

They stumbled across the barren sheets of snow. After a while, the chimneys of buildings rose into view. Their roofs were covered in snow, but their red brick walls stood out in stark contrast against the pale background.

They reached the statue. It towered over them. Vesuvius was cast out of steel, holding his skull cane high in the air. Huge icicles hung from his arms.

'Creepy,' Dan said. 'Why would any town want a statue of Vesuvius, I wonder?'

'They're obviously scared of him,' Poppy said. 'The most powerful leaders are always the most feared. I think Oran was right. We need to be very careful about who we talk to here.'

'Hey, look,' Andrew said, pointing to a sign blowing

on two chains in the wind. It had an arrow pointing ahead saying, 'Nusquam Town'. He hurried toward it. 'Come on, we must be really close.'

The wind carried faint noises of people talking, children playing and market sellers bartering. It didn't sound too dissimilar to home. They turned into a cobbled square that had been dusted with salt.

'Wow,' Andrew said as he gazed at the shops, stalls and people. In the middle was a fountain with a statue of a Shadowmare. The water was coming out of its mouth, but it had completely frozen.

It all looked quite old-fashioned, almost Victorian-looking, Andrew thought, compared to what the Dream Factory was like. The lamp posts were black and gothic, and the small shops were covered in beams with big windows separated into many different tiny sections.

'Mr Basset's Weather Emporium,' one shop sign read. Another, with a blue roof above it, said 'Lucky Charms'. Outside, there were many different baskets. One contained what looked like rabbits' feet, another had four-leafed clovers and the next had tiny pots of gold in it.

'Need some luck?' a woman said, sneaking up behind Andrew and making him jump. She spoke in a foreign accent, which sounded like a cross between Spanish and something he'd never heard before. Andrew turned around. Her dark, curly hair tumbled over her shoulders and down to her waist. 'Can I interest you in a pot of gold from the end of the rainbow? Sourced by myself, the wonderful Madam Voosrer. Only four tallops a pot. Or how about a nice eyeball necklace for the pretty lady?' she asked, trying to put a gold chain around Poppy's neck. 'That'll cost you fifteen tallops.'

'Yuck,' Poppy said, stepping away. 'No thanks. We're fine.'

'Strange, most of the young ladies around here adore them. But suit yourself. Come back if you change your mind.'

'We will,' Andrew said, dragging Poppy away. 'Stay close,' he whispered. 'And try not to talk to anyone.'

'Who are we looking for again?' Dan asked.

But Andrew barely heard him. He was staring at a fish stall. Except it wasn't selling fish at all, but strange octopus-like creatures with twenty legs or more.

'Come buy your fresh seafood here, people,' the man was shouting. 'Lovely juicy mermen tails, three-headed sea monster fins, giant squid tentacles. Buy one get one free.'

'Earth to Andrew,' Dan said in a robot voice. 'Are you even listening? Who's the man we're searching for?'

'Oh,' Andrew said, turning to face them. 'His name's Moonsnake Bill.'

'Moonsnake Bill,' Poppy said dryly. 'Of course. How could I forget a name like *that*? Well, come on then, he must be around here somewhere.'

The man at the fish stall looked up. 'You're looking for Moonsnake Bill?' he said, and then laughed.

'What's so funny?' Andrew asked.

'If you knew him, you'd know where'd he'd be.' He turned and pointed to a dark brown building with a wooden door. 'In there.'

'Thanks,' Andrew said. The building had 'The Merry Drinkers' written above it in big white letters. He guessed it was some sort of pub.

'Do you want to buy some fish?' the man asked.

'What? No thanks,' Andrew said, trying to get past.

The man coughed, stepping in front of him. He rubbed his greasy fingers together.

Poppy nudged him in the rib. 'Give him a tip.'

'Oh, right,' Andrew said. 'Sorry.' He reached into his pocket and pulled out a note. 'Here,' he said. 'Take this.'

The man took the note, eyeing it suspiciously.

'Thanks,' he said, grinning with a set of false teeth. 'Be seeing you soon, then.'

'Well, that was easy,' Dan said, as they crossed the cobbled square.

'How much did you give him?' Poppy asked.

'Ten sacks.' Andrew said. 'However much that is.'

They pushed through the crowd until they came to The Merry Drinkers. Andrew pushed the heavy door open, holding it back for Poppy and Dan.

The pub was full of tables and bar stools. It was dark and dingy, with a metal chandelier hanging from the ceiling, casting a dim glow over everything. There was a bar reaching from one end of the room to the other, with a few old men sitting at it drinking and laughing.

A grouchy-looking landlord stood behind the bar cleaning glasses.

Andrew walked up to him. 'Excuse me,' he said.

Silence. 'Excuse me,' he said again, much louder this time.

The man looked up, studying Andrew with his dark eyes. He was a large man with a round belly that hung over his trousers, bursting through the buttons of his shirt.

He raised a bushy eyebrow and sneered. 'What do you want?'

Andrew kept eye contact. 'I was wondering if you could tell us where Moonsnake Bill is.'

'I'm not even sure if Moonsnake Bill could tell you where he is,' the bartender said, and the men sitting drinking at the bar roared with laughter. The bartender nodded his head towards the end of the bar. 'That's him. Don't say I didn't warn you, though.'

A man with grey knotted hair was asleep face down on the bar, snoring as loud as a boar. He was still clutching a half-empty pint of bright green liquid in his hand.

'Great,' Dan said. 'Oran's friend who is supposed to help us...is a drunk.'

'OK,' Poppy said. 'It's not the best of scenarios, I agree. But it could be worse. We'll just have to wake him up.'

They wandered over to the end of the bar. Poppy tapped him on the back. She flicked his ears. Still no movement. 'Hmm,' she said. 'He's out for the count. This could be harder than I thought.' She tried to remove the glass from Moonsnake Bill's hand. He grunted loudly and sat up.

'Who – what? Thieves!' he yelled, pulling a short sword from his boot.

'Wait,' Andrew said, putting his hands in the air.

180

'We're not thieves. We just want to talk to you.'

Moonsnake Bill cast a wary eye at Andrew, gripping his drink tightly in one hand and his sword in the other. 'Alright,' he slurred. 'What d'yer want?'

'Oran sent us. He told us to come and see you,' Andrew said quickly.

Moonsnake Bill snapped to life, sitting up straight on his stool. 'Oran sent you?'

Poppy nodded. 'Yes. He said you'd help us.'

The man laughed. 'Well I never! How is the old devil?' He downed the rest of his pint in one go, burping loudly when he'd finished.

'He's…' Andrew glanced away, unable to look Moonsnake Bill in the eye. 'He's no longer with us.'

'He's dead?' Moonsnake Bill said, frowning. Andrew flinched at the bluntness of the word.

'Yes. I'm really sorry to have to tell you like this but…'

Moonsnake Bill erupted into laughter, slamming his fists against the bar top.

Andrew took a step back, shocked. Angry. 'What's funny about that? Why are you laughing?'

'He's sick in the head, that's why,' Poppy spat. 'Come on, let's go. We don't need his help.'

They turned to leave.

'Wait,' Moonsnake Bill said, stifling a hiccup. 'I'm sorry. It's just, we had a deal.'

'Huh?' Dan said.

'Oran and I. We had a deal. If I died before him, he'd come to Nusquam Town and run my shop. And if he died before me, well, he mentioned that one day some teenagers might come calling, and if they did, it was my responsibility to help them. It's almost like… he knew. Don't you think?'

'Maybe,' Andrew said. He wouldn't be at all surprised if Oran had planned this.

'So you have to help us?' Poppy said. 'You're obliged to?'

Moonsnake grinned. 'It would seem that way, wouldn't it?' He slapped his hand down on the counter. 'One more drink please, Ralphforus. This is going to be a long day.'

'What are you drinking anyway?' Andrew said, peering into Moonsnake's glass. It appeared to have some kind of green residue in the bottom of it. 'Is it alcohol?'

'Alcohol?' Moonsnake said. 'Good heavens, no. This is beetle juice.'

Dan shook his head. 'Sorry. Did I just hear you correctly? Because I just thought you said beetle juice, and, well, that would be completely gross.'

Moonsnake laughed. 'It's the best drink in all the land. You should try some. It makes your head feel all warm and fuzzy. And you sort of…forget things.' He ran a finger through his knotted hair. 'What was I doing again? Oh yes, ordering more drink.'

'No,' Andrew said quickly. He called the bartender over. 'Better make his next one a coffee, please.'

'With a dash of beetle juice,' Moonsnake Bill added.

Andrew shook his head, and Moonsnake grunted.

'You need to keep a clear head if you're going to help us,' Andrew said. He pulled the wad of cash from his pocket. 'This one's on me.'

'What are you doing? Where did you get all that money from?' Moonsnake Bill asked. 'Quick, put it away before someone sees you! You can't just go flashing big sacks like that around here.'

'Sorry,' Andrew said, shoving the money back in his pocket.

'Not all of it,' Moonsnake said. 'I'll keep this one.' He smiled and plucked a note from the pile.

The bartender placed a steaming hot mug of coffee on the bar. Moonsnake Bill picked it up and brought it to his lips.

'Maybe you should wait for that to cool down a bit first,' Poppy said.

'Nonsense. Mouth like asbestos, see?' He downed the mug in one and jumped from the bar stool, towering over them. 'Right, follow me then.'

'Do you think this is a good idea?' Dan whispered, as they followed Moonsnake out of the pub. 'I mean, he's basically insane.'

Andrew grinned. 'Guess we'll soon find out.'

18

They left the bar and crossed the cobbled square, turning into a narrow street.

Moonsnake Bill stopped at a shop with a blue door. Along the top of the shop were rusty blue letters that spelt, 'Whatever you neep'. Andrew thought it was probably supposed to read 'Whatever you need', but the letter *d* had come loose and was hanging upside down.

Moonsnake Bill pushed the door open and they stepped inside. Andrew gasped at the mess. And Mum thought *his* room was bad! It looked like a junkyard, full of people's unwanted rubbish. Things were stacked on top of shelves and on the floor, and there were even clothes and other items draped over the stair rail at the back of the shop. Andrew glanced at the shelf nearest to him, and saw a pair of Wellington boots with a hole in one of the soles, a tin-opener, a plug without anything attached to it, a pack of playing cards and an old record player.

'Yep, definitely insane,' Andrew muttered.

'What is this place?' Dan asked, holding up an old banana skin with a tag attached to it which read 'Emma's banana.'

'It's my shop,' Moonsnake Bill smiled. He frowned. 'I can't believe you've never heard of it before.'

'Your shop?' Andrew said. 'No offence, Moonsnake, but why would anyone buy any of this junk?'

'Oh, believe me, it *seems* like junk to you, but it all has its uses for the right person. What are your names? I may have something for you.'

'We told you. We're Andrew, Poppy and Dan,' Andrew said, not quite understanding. 'But I don't get—'

'Yes, I remember now,' Moonsnake Bill interrupted, rushing over to a shiny metal chute next to a tall wardrobe. 'How could I forget such strange names?'

'We haven't got strange names,' Poppy said, folding her arms. 'You're the one with the strange—'

'*Shh!*' Andrew said, squeezing her arm. 'Don't upset him. We don't know what he might do.'

Moonsnake Bill spun around holding a small parcel. 'A delivery came for you earlier today.'

'A delivery? For us?' Andrew said. 'Who from? Oran?'

Moonsnake Bill laughed. 'Oh, good heavens, no.

That's just ridiculous. No, the universe, of course.'

Dan coughed. 'The universe?'

'Yes.' Moonsnake Bill nodded, quite serious. He dug his hand inside the parcel. 'Here we are,' he said, pulling out a few bars of candy. 'This is for you.'

'Chocolate?' Dan said. 'Cool. I needed some more of that.'

'Told you,' Moonsnake Bill said, winking.

'Hang on,' Poppy said. 'That's just stupid. Nobody *needs* chocolate. Can't you give him something more useful?'

'Hey,' Dan said. 'Don't argue with the universe. If it wants to give me chocolate, who are we to judge?'

Poppy rolled her eyes. 'Fine. Whatever. We're wasting time. Mum's locked up in some Fear Farm back on Earth and we're here with this loony. And no, Andrew, I won't bite my tongue. It needs to be said.'

'A loony?' Moonsnake Bill said, laughing. 'I wouldn't call your friend Dan a loony. He's just a bit odd.'

'I wasn't talking about Da—' Poppy began to say, but Andrew gave her a look and she stopped mid sentence. 'Look, I just don't get how the universe can send us parcels. It's not a mailman. It doesn't make any sense.'

Moonsnake Bill stopped rummaging through

the boxes and looked up. 'The universe is alive. It has an energy field just like you and I and it *knows* when people need things. My shop simply acts as a distribution centre.' He pointed to a metal chute over by the wardrobe. 'That's where the deliveries come in.'

Dan went and stood under the chute, holding his hands together as if he was praying. 'Look universe, I really need a million pounds. I well need some new Xbox games and I could really do with some new clothes too.' He waited, and then turned to Moonsnake Bill. 'It isn't working,' he said.

Moonsnake Bill laughed again. 'No, of course it isn't. The universe only helps people when they really *need* it.' He began searching through the boxes to his left. 'Where's Poppy's? I can't seem to find it anywhere,' he muttered. 'Oh yes, I remember.' He leapt across the room and began riffling through a laundry basket over by the till. 'Here,' he said, pulling out a pocket mirror and handing it to Poppy. 'This is for you. I'm sure this will come in very handy indeed.'

Poppy took the mirror. 'Err, thanks?' she said, tucking it in her pocket. 'Again, absolutely necessary, I'm sure...'

'Oh yes,' Moonsnake Bill said. 'Definitely necessary.' He spun around so that he was facing Andrew.

'Invisibility potion,' he said. 'And a glowing light.'

'What?'

'Yes. If only I could remember where I put them…' He scratched his head, peering around the shop. 'Ah, here we go.' He pulled out a parcel from underneath a sofa cushion.

Andrew Lake, it said on the front in neat black handwriting. *Well, at least the universe had spelt his name correctly*, Andrew thought with a grin. He tore it open and pulled out a glowing ball of light.

'What is that?' Dan said.

It was shimmering in the palm of Andrew's hand, and rippling as if it was alive.

'No idea,' Moonsnake said. 'Check the parcel. I think there's something else in there.'

Andrew reached into the paper bag again. He pulled out a small glass bottle. He held it up to the light and read the label.

'*Invisibility potion. One minute of invisibility for each sip taken. Do not use if pregnant or under the age of ten.*'

'Hang on, that's not fair,' Dan said, folding his arms. 'How come he gets that?'

'Does this stuff actually work?' Andrew asked.

'Well, of course it works. Haven't you ever used it before?'

'We don't exactly have this back on Earth,' Andrew laughed.

Moonsnake Bill's face suddenly froze. 'Oh my. You're…*human*?'

'Yeah,' Andrew said. 'Last time I checked.'

Moonsnake Bill turned deathly white. He sprinted over to the door and locked it, then leapt over to the window and drew the curtains.

'Is there a problem?' Poppy asked.

'Yes. Oh dear, a terrible problem. Humans are not welcome here in Nusquam.' He scratched his head. 'I hope you didn't draw too much attention to yourself in The Merry Drinkers. How long have you been here?'

'A few hours.'

'And who have you talked to?'

'Let's see,' Andrew said, chewing on his nail. 'We met a lady selling lucky charms, and a fishmonger who we gave some money to for helping us find you. And the barman.'

'How much did you give him?'

'Huh? Who?'

'The fishmonger.'

'Oh. I don't know, one of those notes. Ten sacks, I think.'

'Ten sacks? Oh dear,' Moonsnake Bill said, shaking his head. 'That's an awful lot of money for a Nusquarium child to be carrying around on them. I bet it seemed suspicious. Did he see the rest?'

Andrew bit his lip, shrugging. 'I'm not sure. Maybe.'

Moonsnake Bill paced up and down the room several times. 'It's alright. I'm probably worrying over nothing. You should be fine.'

'What do you mean, *should* be fine? What's wrong?' Poppy said.

'Vesuvius warned us that anyone found harbouring humans would be killed. And anyone that helps to capture one will be rewarded with 1,000 sacks. You're not safe here. And neither am I.'

Andrew gulped as somebody thumped on the door from outside.

19

'Quick!' Moonsnake Bill said. 'Drink the invisibility potion and hide.'

Andrew looked at the strange bottle in his hands. It could have been anything – beetle juice, poison even – but Oran had insisted that they trust Moonsnake Bill with their lives. And Andrew trusted Oran completely.

There was another round of thumps on the door. 'Open up!' a voice yelled from outside. 'Now.'

'Alright, alright. Don't get your knickers in a twist. I'm coming,' Moonsnake Bill said, wandering as slowly as he could over to the door. He looked at Andrew, Poppy and Dan. 'If you want to live, I suggest you drink up.'

'OK,' Andrew said, unscrewing the bottle. He took seven sips and then passed it to Poppy and Dan, who quickly did the same. It tasted of nothing. *Was it really invisibility potion or was Moonsnake Bill just having them on?* He placed the bottle back on the shelf. His stomach rumbled, and he felt a bit sick, but apart from that, nothing changed.

'Quick, in there,' Poppy said, pointing to a wardrobe. They hurried over to it and jumped inside, just as the shop door flew open.

'Ah, Mr Grinch, what can I do for you on this wonderful evening?'

'Cut the act, Moonsnake. Why did you take so long to answer the door?'

Andrew shuffled over and peered through the crack in the wardrobe. A tall, skinny man with a moustache, dressed in rich layers of fur and wearing tall leather boots, paced around the room. 'There's been humans spotted in the area. Two boys and a girl, and with a man matching your description, I might add.'

'Oh?' Moonsnake Bill said innocently. 'I wouldn't know anything about that, Mr Grinch.'

'No?' Mr Grinch said. He spoke in a nasal voice, like he had a cold. 'I had a feeling you'd say that. You won't mind if my men search your premises then?'

Moonsnake shrugged. 'Makes no difference to me.'

'Nuts, Bolt, come on through,' Mr Grinch said. Two burly men with biceps the size of boulders charged inside. They began raiding through baskets, checking behind the curtains and under the stairs.

Andrew peered down at his arms and legs. They were starting to disappear. Nothing but air, all the way up to his elbows. He glanced at Poppy and Dan, who looked like two floating torsos, their limbs completely invisible.

'Whoa,' he breathed. 'Incredible.'

But being *half* invisible wasn't going to save them if Nuts and Bolt decided to look inside the wardrobe. He needed the potion to hurry up and work.

Nuts and Bolt were turning everything over, leaving nothing untouched. It wouldn't be long before they discovered them. Andrew glanced down at his body again. Patches of his skin were still showing, but fading rapidly as the potion started to take effect.

Bolt reached for the wardrobe door.

Andrew froze, his breath catching in his throat.

'Wait,' Moonsnake Bill said. The two men stopped what they were doing. 'You must be thirsty. All this hard work. Come into the back for just a minute and I'll make you boys a cup of tea—'

'No,' Mr Grinch said, his moustache twitching irritably. 'Stop trying to stall them, Moonsnake. I know your game, and it won't work. Bolt, carry on searching. Nuts, check upstairs.'

Nuts nodded and hurried upstairs. Bolt reached for the wardrobe door again.

It flew open. Andrew held his breath, trying to keep

as still and silent as possible, hoping that he was fully invisible.

'Well?' Mr Grinch asked.

'Nothing in there either,' Bolt said, closing the door again.

Andrew let out a sigh of relief.

'You know where they are,' Mr Grinch said. 'I can see it in your eyes.' His head snapped round to where Andrew had left the invisibility potion. 'Aha,' he said, picking it up. Andrew felt his heart drop to the pit of his stomach.

'What are you doing with this? Did you give it to the humans?'

Moonsnake glared at him. 'Of course I didn't. I needed to dodge a debt collector earlier so I used it on myself. They're always hassling me about the damn rent on this place.' He nodded towards a pile of letters on the mat, with big red letters on them saying 'Overdue'.

Mr Grinch twisted his moustache. 'Hmm,' he said. 'Very well. But if we don't find them then, mark my words, Moonsnake, I will be back. You can count on it.'

'Oh, I don't doubt it.'

Mr Grinch grunted and turned back to Nuts and Bolt.

'Move on to the next house. We're wasting our time here.' He turned and stormed out of the shop. Nuts and Bolt hurried after him.

Andrew, Poppy and Dan came tumbling out of the wardrobe.

'Where are you?' Moonsnake whispered.

'Here,' Andrew said.

'I still can't see you.'

Andrew grabbed a straw hat from the shelf and popped it on his head. Poppy and Dan each slid on a pair of shades. 'Better?'

'Not really. I forgot you don't know how to make yourselves visible again. The potion will wear off soon anyway, but if you can close your eyes and think happy thoughts, it'll speed up the process. I don't know why but it works every time.'

'Happy thoughts?' Andrew said doubtfully.

Moonsnake Bill nodded.

'OK.' Andrew shut his eyes and took himself back to three years ago, when he was holidaying in Spain. He thought about lying on a beach while the sun beat down on him and the wind prickled his skin. For a second he almost got lost in the moment, and had to pinch himself back to reality.

'See? Told you,' Moonsnake said.

Andrew looked down at his arms and legs. It had worked!

'Follow me upstairs. You had better explain to me what you're doing here,' Moonsnake Bill said.

They hurried after him. The upstairs of his house was small, just a bedroom, a bathroom and a kitchen, but surprisingly it was quite neat and tidy compared to the shop below. Moonsnake took out a bottle of beetle juice from the fridge and poured himself a glass. He slumped into an armchair, farting loudly.

Poppy covered her nose and Dan laughed loudly.

'Sorry, only got the one chair. Not used to having visitors. You'll have to find a cushion and sit on the floor.'

'Charming,' Poppy muttered.

'That's OK,' Andrew said, crouching down.

'So, what brings you here?' Moonsnake asked, taking a sip from his glass and letting out a contented sigh.

'The Dreamsphere; do you know what that is?' Andrew asked.

'Yes, of course I do. It's the place where old dreams and nightmares are stored. It's run by a greedy, conniving man called Grimble Whatt. He makes his living by charging Nusquariums hundreds of sacks to go and get plugged into a dream because we're unable to dream ourselves.' He paused, finishing his drink. 'But why would you be interested in that?'

'We're not,' Poppy said. 'We're here to find the Fender's Feather. Oran thought it might be hidden in the Dreamsphere.'

'Of course,' Moonsnake Bill said, nodding. 'Quite possible. But there's no way you'd actually get inside the Dreamsphere. Nobody but Vesuvius and Grimble is allowed to go inside. We're only allowed in the dreaming lounge.'

'We're hoping we might be able to bribe him,' Dan said.

'So that's what all this money's for then? Well, it's certainly worth a go. But do you realise how dangerous it'll be? The Dreamsphere is not a place to be messed with.'

'Well we didn't exactly expect it to be a walk in the park. Oran warned us it would be dangerous, but we have no choice,' Dan said. 'Our world is in danger and this is the only way to save it.'

'Can you take us there?' Andrew asked.

Moonsnake Bill poured himself another glass of beetle juice. He downed it in one this time.

'No. I promised Oran I'd look after you. And that

is exactly what I shall do.' He got up and hurried into the bedroom. There was a clattering noise and he came back minutes later with a bag slung over his shoulder. He picked up the half-drunk bottle of beetle juice. 'If you're absolutely intent on going inside the Dreamsphere, then I'm coming with you.'

'We're going now?' Dan said.

'No time like the present,' Moonsnake said. 'Besides, if we stay here any longer, I fear Mr Grinch will have your heads on a stick.'

20

Moonsnake handed them each a backpack. 'Take these,' he said. 'I've put a few items in them which might come in handy.'

'Thanks,' Andrew said, slinging it on his shoulder.

Dan was standing by the chute. 'Hey, Poppy,' he said. 'There's a parcel here for you. And one for someone else too.'

'A parcel for me?' Poppy said, raising an eyebrow.

'Oh, good, a delivery,' Moonsnake said, hurrying over. 'Let's see what the universe has sent us today, shall we?'

They crowded around eagerly.

Dan handed Poppy the parcel. It was a small box. She opened it and peered inside.

Andrew leaned over her shoulder. 'What is it?'

She pulled it out. 'I don't know,' she said, puzzled. 'It looks like a light bulb.'

'Not a light bulb,' Moonsnake said. 'A dark bulb. It's black, see?'

'What the hell is a dark bulb?' Dan said dryly. 'Or

should I not even ask?'

'It's the opposite of a light bulb. Instead of giving out light, it makes everything dark.'

'Oh,' Poppy said, frowning. 'I don't understand why I'd need one of them. I hate the dark, but if you say so, Moonsnake.'

'It's not I who says so,' Moonsnake said. 'It is the universe. Who's the other parcel for?'

It was extremely long and thin. Andrew turned it over and studied the label carefully. 'Billabong Flewsbry Bloom. Who's that?'

'It's me,' Moonsnake said, turning red. 'Yes, bit of a mouthful, isn't it?'

'That's your name?' Dan said, laughing hysterically. 'Ha. No wonder everyone calls you Moonsnake Bill.' He paused. 'Hang on. Why *do* they call you that?'

'Because I used to fight Moonsnakes in bar competitions. I was world champion for a while, best in Nusquam.'

'Moonsnakes?' Andrew said. 'And they would be what, exactly?'

'A snake with three heads,' Moonsnake replied, as if it was obvious.

'Oh, OK then.'

'So, what's in your parcel?' Poppy asked.

'I have no idea,' Moonsnake said, shaking it. He ripped it open and pulled out a steel sword, decorated with red rubies.

'Wow,' Dan said. 'Now *that* is one cool-looking sword.'

'I agree,' Moonsnake said. 'I already have a pretty good one, but you can never have enough swords, in my opinion.' He shoved it in his left boot. 'Oh, and you may want to finish up that invisibility potion before we leave,' Moonsnake Bill said as he rose to his feet. 'The town will be on red alert by now.'

Andrew nodded. He pulled the bottle from his backpack and took a few gulps, then handed it to Poppy and Dan.

'Are you going to take some too?' Andrew asked Moonsnake.

'Me? No. I'll be fine. You'll need me to get inside the Dreamsphere, and I won't be able to if I'm invisible.'

When the potion had taken full effect, Moonsnake Bill opened the door of the shop and peered outside.

'OK, it's safe. Get moving,' he said, shooing them out.

They ventured out into the freezing cold. Darkness pressed in on them, and the streetlamps offered little light as they crept down the narrow cobbled street. Two heavily built guards stood at the entrance of the square, cradling axes.

Andrew gulped, eyeing the sharpened blades uneasily.

'Evening, fellas,' Moonsnake said.

'Where are you off to?' one of the guards asked.

Moonsnake laughed, and stumbled back slightly. Andrew wondered if he was doing it on purpose. 'I'm off to The Merry Drinkers. Where else?'

The taller of the two guards sighed. 'Let him past, Rudnick. He's a harmless drunk. What would he be doing smuggling humans?'

The other guard laughed. 'You're right,' he said, stepping aside to let Moonsnake past. Andrew, Poppy and Dan hurried closely behind him.

They headed in the direction of The Merry Drinkers, and as soon as the guards weren't looking, turned down another alleyway, which was engulfed in darkness.

'We're here,' Moonsnake whispered.

'Where?' Andrew said, looking around. He couldn't see anything.

'The entrance to the Dreamsphere,' Moonsnake whispered. He clicked his torch on, and the alleyway was filled with a soft light. He knocked on an old, metal door, which was rusty with age.

'You sure this is it, man?' Dan whispered. 'It doesn't look like somewhere dreams would be kept. It looks like a dump.'

'Positive,' Moonsnake said.

After a few seconds, the door eased open a crack.

'What do you want?' a grouchy voice asked from the other side.

'I'd like to buy a dream,' Moonsnake said.

The door opened a little wider, revealing a bald man with thin spectacles. 'You?' he said, with a puzzled expression. 'Sorry. I'm only open to regular customers tonight. Vesuvius has the place on high security alert.'

'I know,' Moonsnake whispered. 'But I'm desperate, Grimble, please.'

'Sorry, no can do,' the man said, closing the door.

Moonsnake quickly stuck his foot inside. He reached into his bag and pulled out half the wad of cash. 'I'd be willing to pay generously.'

Grimble eyed the money hungrily, as if considering the offer. 'Give it here,' he said, snatching it from Moonsnake. 'Follow me, and turn that light off.'

He opened the door up wide enough for Moonsnake to enter. Andrew, Poppy and Dan followed quickly behind him, slipping inside just in time, before Grimble slammed the door shut again. They walked up a very long, very narrow passageway. Andrew had no idea where they were heading.

Finally Grimble stopped and lit a lantern. They were outside another grubby-looking door. Grimble took out a key from his pocket and placed it in the lock. When the door sprang open, a dazzling light blinded them. They stepped into a large hall, with a plush red carpet. The cream walls were covered in ornate plaster decorations. A glittering chandelier hung from above.

'Follow me into my office,' Grimble said, and they walked straight into a room on the right.

He sat at his desk, looking small in his oversized leather chair.

'What do you want, Moonsnake? Everybody knows you don't have a penny to your name and you spend what you do have getting sozzled on beetle juice. So come on, tell me, where did you get all that money from and what do you want?'

'We want to get inside the Dreamsphere,' Moonsnake said.

Grimble sat tapping his fingers on the desk. He stopped suddenly. 'We?'

Great, thought Andrew. Moonsnake had given the

game away. Slowly, Andrew let his arms and legs, and then his body, fade back into view. Poppy and Dan did the same.

'Oh,' Grimble said. 'I see.' He put his hand underneath the desk, patting around.

'Stop. What are you doing?' Andrew said, hurrying over to him. 'You better not be searching for the alarm button.'

Grimble shot up from his seat. 'Stand back, human. Don't come any closer. I'm calling Vesuvius.'

21

'Wait,' Andrew said. 'Please, just hear us out first.'

Grimble moved his hand away from the alarm button slightly. 'I'm listening.'

'We need this. We need to find the Fender's Feather and stop Vesuvius.'

Grimble let out a nasal laugh. 'Vesuvius hid the feather inside a dream he created, and then paid *me* to store it inside the Dreamsphere. Why would I let you enter?' He snorted. 'Vesuvius would have me killed for that.'

'Please, Grimble.' Andrew said, tears filling his eyes. He could feel desperation running through his veins. 'Do the right thing. If you don't help us, my world ends. Everybody I care about dies.'

'I'm not interested in becoming a hero, human,' Grimble said. He reached for the button again.

'We have something to give you,' Andrew said. 'In exchange.'

'All right, I'm intrigued. What could you possibly

have that I would want badly enough to risk my own life for?'

'This,' Andrew said, reaching into his bag.

Grimble flinched slightly. 'It's OK, it's not a weapon,' Andrew said, taking the small glass vial out. 'Oran made it for you. I think it's a dream.'

Grimble's eyes widened and he stood up. 'The lovelost dream?'

Andrew nodded. 'Err…yeah. Whatever that is.'

'Give it to me.' Grimble reached his hand out like an eager child.

Andrew drew back. 'Not until you've got us safely inside the Dreamsphere.'

Grimble scratched his head. 'I've been asking Oran for years to make me that dream.' He shook his head. 'But I can't. Vesuvius would murder me if he knew I let you inside the Dreamsphere.'

'Then you don't get this,' Andrew said, holding up the glass vial. 'Oran's dead, Grimble. He left us this to bargain with you, but I could smash it right now if—'

'Wait,' Grimble said, his eyes fixed hungrily on the vial in Andrew's hands. 'Alright, I'll let you inside. And I'll give you a head start of two hours before I raise the alarm.'

'Three,' Moonsnake said.

'Can't do that. Vesuvius would get too suspicious. Two and a half. Final offer. I'm not telling you which dream the feather is hidden inside either. That's up to you to find out.'

'OK,' Andrew said. 'Deal.'

'Good,' Grimble said, with a slight smile. 'Follow me.'

They walked back into the main hall and up a set of wide steps. There were lots of beds lined up against the walls, like a hospital, with men and women fast asleep on them. They had wires attached to every part of their bodies, which lead to a drip at the side of each bed, containing colourful liquid.

'What are they doing?' Dan asked.

'*Shh!*' Grimble said. 'They're dreaming. Each drip contains a dream and it's slowly fed into their bodies. They can touch, taste, and move around in their dreams just like you and I can in real life. It's quite extraordinary.'

Andrew shivered. It reminded him of the Fear Pods at the Nightmare Factory. 'So people actually choose to come here?' he said, unable to get his head around the idea.

'Well, of course they do, strange boy. And they pay good money too. Only the very wealthy can afford to buy dreams. The rarer the dream, the more it costs. And to think, you humans get to dream every single night…for free. You don't realise how lucky you are,' Grimble said with a degree of jealousy.

'Yeah, but we get nightmares too,' Dan said. 'That's no fun.'

Grimble ignored him, stopping at a door at the end of the room. Two guards stood in front of it.

'Evening, boss,' one of the guards said. 'What about the children and the man? Are they waiting outside?'

'They're OK, they're with me,' Grimble said. 'Let them pass.'

The guard raised his eyebrows, but then stepped aside.

They followed Grimble down another very long and straight passageway, much lighter than the first one. They reached a metal door at the end, with a keypad affixed to the wall.

Grimble typed in a code, and the door clicked open. They stepped inside, walking onto a wooden platform with a pier leading off it. Andrew put a hand to his mouth, lost for words. They were inside a vast sphere. It was pitch black except for thousands of floating, glowing orbs, twinkling and revolving like planets.

'It's like looking into space,' Andrew said, when he'd finally mustered the ability to speak. He looked down, head spinning, realising that he was standing only inches away from a deep drop into the abyss.

'It's beautiful,' Poppy said, gazing up.

'Thank you.' Grimble smiled, but it quickly turned into a sneer. 'You better enjoy it whilst you can. Vesuvius will be after you soon, that's if you haven't perished in the Dreamsphere already.'

'Charming man, isn't he?' Moonsnake said.

'Grimble, do you mind if I ask you something?' Andrew said.

'Yes, I do mind. But I suspect you're going to ask anyway, so go ahead.'

'What dream did Oran give you? What was so special about it?'

Grimble sighed, as if considering whether or not to tell them. 'Not that it's any of your business, but it's a dream that allows people to see their loved ones when they have passed over. I want to see my wife again,' he said, almost sounding human for a moment. 'Plus I can make lots more money from it.' He rubbed his hands together greedily, and then checked his watch. 'Right, you have two and a half hours starting from now. Use the machine by the door to select what

211

dream you wish to enter. The password is "Elbmirg"

Poppy grinned. 'That's Grimble backwards, isn't it?'

Grimble nodded. 'Clever girl. A lot of things are backwards in the Dreamsphere, and you'll need a brain like yours to get you through.'

Poppy smiled, blushing.

'Good luck; you're going to need it,' Grimble sneered, opening the door. He disappeared back into the corridor and the door slammed shut behind him, leaving them all alone.

'Two and a half hours,' Dan said, setting his watch. 'That isn't long, man. We'd better get a move on if we're going to find that feather.'

To the left of the door was a machine, which looked like an old Eighties computer and a keyboard.

'Someone else better do this,' Moonsnake said. 'I'm hopeless at technology.'

'I've got it covered,' Andrew said.

He stepped in front of the computer, and a message popped up on the screen, as if it could sense their presence.

Hello.

Password?

'Elbmirg', Andrew typed in, careful not to make any mistakes.

Almost as soon as he had finished typing, another message flashed up on the screen.

Password accepted.

Please select dream search.

'What should I write back?' Andrew said.

'Try *feathers*,' Moonsnake said. 'We're searching for a dream with a feather in it.'

Andrew typed 'feathers' in. The computer made a strange whirring sound.

'Hey, look, guys,' Dan said, pointing into the Dreamsphere. 'Some of the orbs are disappearing.'

Thousands of the glowing balls were blinking out, as if they were spotlights being turned off one by one. Only a few lights remained shining. They floated down towards where they were standing.

The computer beeped. Andrew turned back around to find another message on the screen.

Two thousand dreams with 'Feathers' found.

'Hmm,' Moonsnake said, stroking his chin. 'That's still too many to choose from. We need to narrow it down a bit more. Try typing in "Feathers" and "Vesuvius".'

'OK,' Andrew said, hitting the keyboard again. The computer groaned and buzzed, and the Dreamsphere suddenly became very dark.

Another beep.

Two dreams with 'Feathers' and 'Vesuvius' found.

Please select dream.

Andrew turned around. There were two orbs floating in front of them, wrapped in purple light and blinding to look at.

'Which one do you think contains the Fender's Feather?' Andrew asked.

'No idea,' Moonsnake said. 'I suppose we'll just have to guess.'

'But we'll know if we pick the wrong one, won't we?' Poppy said. 'Because it won't contain any traps.'

'Not necessarily,' Moonsnake said. 'The fake dream could be booby-trapped, so we wouldn't know either way until the very end.'

'Marvellous,' Dan said, shaking his head. 'So which one shall we go for?'

'I vote for the first one,' Poppy said.

'Why's that?' Andrew asked.

'Well, it seems a little duller than the second light, and therefore less alluring. So maybe Vesuvius thought we wouldn't pick it. Secondly, we only have two and a hours left and we can't stand around all day trying to decide which one to go for.'

'You're right,' Andrew said. 'Decision made then. I just hope that it's the right one.' He turned back to the computer and typed, 'Select dream one'.

Dream one selected, the computer flashed back. Then, *Running dream sequence.*

The orb on the right disappeared, while the one on the left expanded. It filled the blackness with a warm, violet glow. At the end of the pier, a door appeared. Andrew walked up to it, the others following closely behind him.

He took a deep breath. 'Here goes,' he said, placing his hand around the doorknob and twisting it. The door creaked open and they stepped inside into a dark room with a very high ceiling. There was a pale glow shining from somewhere in the back.

'Where is that strange light coming from?' Andrew asked.

There was a venomous hiss.

'More importantly, what was that noise?' Dan said, voice shaking.

22

Poppy froze. 'It sounded like a…snake.'

'Not just any snake,' Moonsnake said. 'A Moonsnake snake.'

'Did that just sound strange to anyone else?' Dan said.

Andrew ignored him. 'Huh? The creature you used to fight in bar competitions?'

Moonsnake Bill nodded. 'Pass me my beetle juice,' he said. Andrew took out the bottle from his rucksack and handed it to Moonsnake Bill.

'How will that help kill it?' Andrew asked.

Moonsnake took a large glug from the bottle and handed it back. 'It won't,' he said. 'I just need a drink before I annihilate this thing.'

'What are you going to do?' Poppy asked.

'I'm going to craft me some new boots.' Moonsnake Bill stepped forwards, waving his sword in the air. 'Come on, you slithering reptile. Come and bite me. I dare you.'

The snake slithered out of the crack in the wall,

glowing as if it had radioactive skin. It was a mustard-yellow colour, with three heads. It crawled towards them and uncoiled itself so that its heads reached the ceiling, towering over them.

Poppy froze, swaying from side to side, her eyes turning a misty yellow colour.

'Yo, Poppy,' Dan said, clapping his hands together. 'Earth to Poppy!' He paused. 'Err, Andrew, I think there's something wrong with your sister.'

'What? What's wrong with her?'

'The snake is entrancing her with its many eyes. If you look into them and let the fear take over, it can send you into a state of hypnosis,' Moonsnake said.

'So what do we do?' Andrew asked, feeling his stomach tie up in knots.

'What any good snake fighter does. Drive the fear to the back of your mind. Your sister will return to normal once we have killed it.'

'Right,' Andrew said, nodding. 'Of course.'

The snake lurched forwards. All three mouths snapped open, long red tongues winding out. Each mouth had two pointed fangs, longer than Andrew's body. The snake hissed at them again, and Andrew felt a spray of saliva strike his face. He wiped his eyes.

'Right,' he said, rolling up his sleeves and raising his hands.

'No!' Moonsnake yelled, but Andrew sent blistering green light through the air, hitting the creature in its left head. The head exploded. Green and yellow goo splattered the walls.

'Now look what you've gone and done,' Moonsnake said, burying his face in his hands.

'Huh? I'm killing it. Just like you said to do.'

'Not like that,' Moonsnake said, as Andrew took aim at the second head.

Andrew froze. The stump from the first began to split into two, each section growing steadily until a head popped out from each one.

'What just happened?' Andrew said, counting the heads with his finger. 'There's four of them now.'

Moonsnake Bill sighed. 'With Moonsnakes, every time you destroy a head, two more grow in its place. The only way to kill them is to destroy their eyes.'

'OK, I can do that.' He flexed his fingers again. He tried to aim, but the heads kept on swinging from side to side. He couldn't get a clear shot.

'I'm too far away,' he said.

Moonsnake nodded. 'Exactly.'

'Then how are we supposed to kill it?' Dan asked.

Moonsnake grinned. 'Take this,' he said, pulling out the sword from his left boot and handing it to him.

'Wow,' Dan said, running a hand down its steel blade. 'What do I do with it?'

But Moonsnake Bill was already racing up behind the snake. The heads twisted around all at once, striking at him. Moonsnake weaved in and out, ducking and dodging when the heads got too close. He jumped up onto the snake's back, gripping its scales and climbing up its back. 'This is a little bigger than the ones I've had to fight before,' Moonsnake yelled down to them. 'But it's all the same. Come on up.'

'He's mad,' Dan said. 'What's he playing at?'

'No idea,' Andrew muttered, unable to draw his eyes away.

Moonsnake reached the first head, and crawled onto the snake's nose as the other heads twisted around to try and bite him. He stood up, pulling the second sword from his boot. He swung it about, trying to warn the other snakeheads away.

'We can't let him fight those things on his own,' Andrew said. 'I'm going to climb up and help him.' He ran towards the snake, turning when he reached its tail. 'Dan, are you coming?'

Dan shrugged. 'Sure, why not? Killing giant

glowing snakes is all in a day's work for us now, right?' Dan sprinted over to Andrew as fast as he could. He cupped his hands together and hoisted Andrew up onto the snake's back.

Andrew curled his legs around the snake. It was a bit like mounting a horse. He grabbed hold of the snake's scales as it wriggled around on the floor, twisting and turning to try and shake him off. He could feel its huge muscles pulsating underneath him.

'Here,' he said, extending a hand to Dan and pulling him up. They began climbing the snake's body, using the cracks between its giant scales as footholds.

They reached the part where the snake's body split into four different heads. They were so high up that Poppy was just a tiny blob of colour on the ground.

Dan gulped. 'Did I ever mention that I hate heights?'

'Bit late for that now,' Andrew said, grinning. 'Come on, hurry.'

Moonsnake Bill slid down one of the necks. 'Job done,' he said, holding up his sword. Two yellow snake eyes were stuck on the end of it like a kebab. 'Snake eyes are a delicacy in Nusquam. I'll keep hold of them for later and we'll eat them when we get hungry.'

'*Eww*,' Dan said, grimacing. 'Maybe *you* will.'

Moonsnake grinned. 'One head down, three to go,' he said, running up another neck.

Andrew climbed up one of the heads, as Dan climbed up another.

The other heads lunged at Andrew, fangs clamping down inches away from him as he crawled on his hands and knees up the bucking neck. He glanced at Dan, who was struggling to hold on as the head he was on swung from side to side.

Andrew lunged forwards and pierced the sword into one of its eyes. The snake hissed. He quickly dived sideways and stabbed his sword into the other eye.

A rush of elation pulsed through him. He'd done it. He'd killed one of the snakeheads. He glanced at Moonsnake Bill, who had just finished slaughtering the third. There was just one more to go. He looked at Dan.

'Help!' Dan shouted. He was dangling from the snake's tongue like it was a rope swing.

'What happened?'

'I went for one of the eyes and it jerked forwards. I slid down its nose and I grabbed hold of the only thing I could.' he said, tears streaming down his face. 'I don't want to die.'

'Hang on,' Andrew said. 'I'll get help. Keep holding

on. Don't let go.' He spun around. 'Moonsnake Bill,' he yelled. 'Hey, Moonsnake!'

Moonsnake Bill turned to look at them.

'Oh dear,' he said, his face pale. 'I'm coming. Don't move a muscle.'

'I can't hold on,' Dan cried. 'I'm…. I'm about to fall.'

Dan was sliding down the snake's tongue, losing his grip as it thrashed about madly to try and shake him off. Andrew had to do something, and fast, or else Dan would fall to his death. He fired a bolt of light into one of the snake's eyes. It hissed out in pain, and whipped its head back. Dan screamed. The next few seconds seemed to pass in slow motion. Andrew watched, horrified, as Dan was thrown into the air, plummeting towards the ground. The snake opened up its huge jaws and swooped down for its prey.

'No!' Andrew yelled, as the snake swallowed him up.

Andrew felt anger building inside him. Hatred. Rage. He fired another pulse of energy at the snake's remaining eye. The light hit it square in the pupil, shattering the eye into a million tiny fragments. The snake hissed one final time – but it was too late.

Dan was gone.

23

'Quickly,' Moonsnake yelled. 'Slide down before it collapses.'

'What?' Andrew snapped back to life. He ran, following Moonsnake's lead as he slid down the snake's long, slippery back as if it was a chute. Just as he reached the tail, the luminous glow of the snake's body blinked out, plunging them into darkness.

The snake collapsed to the ground with such force, Andrew and Moonsnake were thrown onto the hard floor, landing on their fronts.

Andrew opened his eyes, the room spinning like a merry-go-round. The snake was lying in a heap on the floor beside them.

'Nice work!' Moonsnake said, getting up. He put his hand up for a high five but Andrew turned away, ignoring him. 'That was impressive. When we've found the Fender's Feather, I could enter you into a few bar fights if you'd like?'

'Dan got eaten. It was all my fault,' Andrew said, swallowing back tears. 'And you want to celebrate?'

Moonsnake Bill bit his lip. 'Sorry,' he said. 'Look, if it makes you feel any better, it was probably a really quick death.'

Andrew gritted his teeth. 'Well it doesn't, alright? It doesn't make me feel better at all.'

Poppy appeared behind Andrew.

'Andrew,' she said, her voice shaking. 'What happened? The last thing I remember was that massive snake with three heads. And now it's on the floor…dead.'

'Yeah,' Andrew said, his voice flat. 'We killed it.'

'That's brilliant!' Poppy said. She sat down next to him. 'Isn't it?'

'Dan's dead,' Andrew said, and he let the tears flow, no longer trying to hold them back. 'First Oran, and now Dan. And it's all my fault.'

'I'm not dead!' a voice said, making Andrew jump.

Andrew sat up, sure that he had imagined it. 'Huh?'

'I said I'm not dead. I'm inside here, you numbnut. Man, it stinks so bad. You gotta get me out of this thing.' The voice echoed as if it was coming from under a bridge. Or…inside a very large snake.

'Dan!' Andrew said, jumping up. He ran to the snake and put his hands up against its scaly skin. 'You're in there?'

'Where else would I be?'

'Impossible.' Moonsnake grinned.

'Are you OK?' Andrew asked.

'Of course I'm not OK. I'm stuck inside a giant snake's guts. Get me out of here. NOW! I can hardly breathe.'

'We're coming,' Andrew said. 'Don't move.'

They raced around to the nearest snakehead. Its jaws were wide open, fangs biting into the ground like two goalposts.

'Do we have to go in there?' Poppy asked, trembling. 'You know I hate snakes. What if it comes alive or something?'

'Snakes can't come back from the dead, Poppy.' Andrew grinned. 'You've got nothing to worry about.'

'OK, fine.' She nodded. 'After you.'

Andrew got on his hands and knees and crawled underneath the huge fangs.

'Come on,' he said, helping Poppy through. Moonsnake Bill came next. He turned on his torch, and shone it into the dark mouth. It looked like a forbidding cave. Andrew stared up. The snake's mouth was red and black. A stench of dead meat lingered in the air, which was almost unbearable.

He grabbed hold of the snake's slippery wet tongue, and used it like a rope to tug himself into the snake's throat. Slimy yellow and red goo streaked the walls and the floor. Andrew trod carefully, trying not to slip.

A gurgling noise rumbled through the body of the snake, like a plughole sucking down water.

'Andrew, I'm scared,' Poppy whispered.

'Here, take my hand,' he said, as they crept forwards together into the darkness. They waded through some sort of liquid, as thick as tar, which soaked their trousers all the way up to their knees. Dan was right – it reeked of sewage in here. Andrew pinched his nose to block out the smell.

'Dan!' he yelled. But there was no reply.

'Where do you think he's gone?' Poppy asked.

'I don't know,' Moonsnake said. 'Let's just keep on looking.'

They trudged through the dark insides of the snake. It reminded Andrew of the tube tunnel where Oran had died, and he sighed hopelessly again, a wave of guilt washing over him.

Then light. A bright light shining from the end.

'What do you think that is?' Andrew said.

'Oh my God, it's the snake,' Poppy said. 'It's coming back to life!'

Moonsnake Bill tilted his head. 'No, it's not that. It's something else.' They crept forwards. The circle of light at the end of the tunnel grew larger. Andrew thought he could see blue patches in it, almost like sky. But that was impossible. They were inside a snake. Nothing was supposed to be at the end but its tail.

'We're in the Dreamsphere,' Moonsnake Bill said, as if reading Andrew's mind. 'Anything is possible.'

Moonsnake Bill shone his torch on the walls. They had turned an earthy brown colour and were textured like rock.

Poppy put a hand to her chin, looking thoughtful. 'It's as if we're in some sort of cave.'

'I think we are,' Andrew said, beginning to run towards the light, towards the opening. The floor beneath him became soft and difficult to run on. He looked down. It was yellow and grainy like...*sand*.

He stumbled to the opening of the cave, into the fresh air, panting hard. Dan was stood at the entrance, looking out. His tall frame was a silhouette against the bright purple sun. *Thank God*, thought Andrew, as he bounded toward him.

'Mate!' Dan said, turning around and patting him on the back. 'Good to see you. Can you believe it?' he said. 'A beach with a clear blue ocean.'

Andrew shook his head. He couldn't. One moment they had been inside a snake, and the next they were looking out onto a beautiful beach. 'I'm glad you're alright,' he said to Dan. 'For a moment, I thought you might have di…' He stopped, choking up.

'Awww,' Dan said, ruffling his hair. 'You were worried about me, weren't you, mate? That's sweet.'

Andrew growled at him, stepping out onto the clean white sand. The dark sea glistened in places as the sun reflected off it in tiny beams of light. Poppy and Moonsnake Bill came running up behind him.

'Who would have thought it?' Moonsnake chuckled. 'That we needed to travel *inside* the snake's mouth?'

'Huh? We were supposed to come down here?' Andrew said.

'Well, yes. Although I'm not sure we would have realised in time if Dan hadn't been eaten.'

'You can thank me later,' Dan said, waving a hand. 'Come on, let's go check it out.'

'Be careful,' Moonsnake said. 'You are still inside the Dreamsphere, remember. Keep a close eye out.'

They walked out onto the beach. A cool breeze blew through the air. It looked like any normal beach, except for the purple sky. But there was something else that was different about this beach, which Andrew couldn't put his finger on.

'It's silent,' he said, after a while. 'Eerily silent.'

228

'Err, that's because nobody is speaking, numbnuts,' Dan said.

'No. I mean, listen.' He stopped, tilting his ear up to the sky. 'There are no birds. No people. Nothing.'

'You're right,' Moonsnake said.

'Don't you think that's a bit odd? I mean, Vesuvius planted this beach here for a reason. And it wasn't so that we could gaze at the scenery. There's obviously something we're missing.'

'Right again,' Moonsnake said. 'But what?'

Andrew walked up to the water's edge. The frothy tide rose up to his feet, crackling on the dry, hot sand. 'I don't know,' he said, hopelessness spreading through him. Then he saw something. A reflection in the water – but not his reflection. A face. A man. He had a pointed nose and a brown beard which was so curly and frazzled, it looked as if it was made from hundreds of worms.

Andrew spun around, but saw no one there.

24

He turned back to the water's edge. Again, Andrew saw the reflection of a man with dark hair and a long wiry beard staring back at him. The reflection blinked and then turned to run.

'Wait,' Andrew said, spinning around. 'I know you're there. Don't leave. I only want to talk to you.' He began to run. He wasn't sure how he planned to chase an invisible man exactly, but right now, he didn't care. This might be his only chance at finding the Fender's Feather.

Then, a glimmer in the air, like dust caught in the light.

'Yes,' Andrew said. 'Don't be afraid. Show yourself.'

'Who are you talking to?' Dan asked. 'Have you gone mad now, too? Is it something in the air?' He covered his nose and mouth.

Andrew didn't say anything. He kept on focusing on the spot where he'd seen the light sparkle.

Slowly, a man appeared. His head reached no higher than Andrew's waist, and he had a round, stout body. His face was so pitted and coarse that it looked like living rock.

'Whoa,' Dan said, jumping when he saw him.

'Not supposed to talk to you,' the man said, pointing a trembling finger at Andrew. 'You're not allowed to be here. The man with black eyes, the one that put me here, he'd kill me if he knew I was talking to you.'

'Vesuvius?' Poppy said, and the small man flinched at the mention of his name. 'Look, it's OK. We're here to stop him. We're here to find the Fender's Feather. Do you know what that is?'

The man nodded. 'It's what I'm supposed to be protecting.'

Moonsnake staggered forward, so suddenly that it made the small man jump several paces backwards. 'Do you know *where* it is?'

'No. The man told me to wait. Only wait, he said. Talk to no one.'

'You can talk to us,' Andrew said. 'We won't tell. What else did Vesuvius say?'

'To let him know if I ever saw strangers come here. Like you.'

'OK,' Andrew said, crouching down on the sand so that he didn't tower over the man. He held out his hand. 'I'm Andrew. My friends here are Poppy, Dan and Moonsnake Bill. See? We're not strangers any more. You can talk to us.'

The man crept forward hesitantly, and then smiled, reaching out to shake Andrew's hand. 'I'm Crinkle,' he said.

'Hey, Crinkle.' Poppy smiled. 'Listen, we need to find the Fender's Feather. It's important. Can you help us?'

Crinkle didn't seem to be paying attention. His eyes were fixed on Dan's trouser pocket. He licked his lips. Dan glanced down at the half-eaten chocolate bar that was sticking out of it.

'You want that?' Andrew asked him. 'It's called chocolate.'

Crinkle bent down on all fours, like a dog, and began sniffing Dan's pocket. He licked his lips and nodded.

'No,' Dan said. 'It's mine. He's not having it.'

Crinkle stood back up, folding his arms. 'Then me not give you answers you need.' He disappeared again.

Dan rolled his eyes and reached into his pocket. He held the chocolate bar out. 'Fine, take it.'

The wrapper fell to the ground and the chocolate bar disappeared in three single bites.

Crinkle reappeared with chocolate smeared all over

his mouth. 'Mmm, me like chocolate. You got more?'

'Yes,' Andrew said. 'But not until you help us out.'

Crinkle frowned. 'But what if evil man finds out? What if he kills me?'

'He won't,' Andrew said. 'Because we're going to kill him first.'

'So will you help us?' Poppy asked.

Crinkle hesitated, and then nodded slowly.

'Good,' Andrew said, standing up. 'We need you to get us out of here. To the next stage of the dream. Can you do that?'

'I get boat,' the man said, and disappeared into the cave at the side of the beach.

'Don't you think we should have gone with him?' Dan said. 'He's probably going to run back and tell Vesuvius now.'

'No,' Andrew said. 'We can trust him, I know we can.'

'Not exactly the brightest bulb in the box though, is he?' Moonsnake said, as Crinkle hurried back, dragging a wooden rowing boat along the jagged rocks. Andrew and Poppy raced over to help him, picking it up so that it wouldn't break.

They set it down on the water and climbed inside. Crinkle picked up an oar and started to row. Andrew picked up the other one and helped him. 'Where are we heading?'

'To the dark forest,' Crinkle said.

Dan laughed dryly. 'Great, because *that* doesn't sound at all dangerous, does it?'

'It is very dangerous,' Crinkle said, not detecting the sarcasm. 'Me not come with you. Me wait on the beach.'

'Funny, I had a feeling he might say that,' Dan muttered.

The water was an inky blue colour, but as they rowed closer towards the island, it began to turn red, frothing against the rocky shore like blood oozing from a wound. Andrew rubbed the goose pimples which had sprouted on his arms, staring up at the forest which loomed over them. It was black and dead-looking, like a graveyard for trees. The blackness seemed to wait for them, as if it wanted to engulf them.

Crinkle pulled the boat up onto the rocks and held out his hand. 'Chocolate now?'

'Fine,' Dan said, pulling out the three remaining bars from his pocket.

'Wait,' Andrew said. 'Tell us where we need to go first.'

'Straight ahead. Find the tree that stands alone. Knock three times on the bark. Now give chocolate?'

Andrew nodded, and Dan handed him the bars, slightly begrudgingly.

'Thank you, Crinkle.' Poppy smiled.

Crinkle walked back to his boat and sat down. 'It's OK. And be careful. Remember, dangerous forest.'

'Yeah, you already said that,' Andrew muttered. *What was in there?* he wondered. What was Crinkle so afraid of?'

They hurried into the sea of trees, keeping close together. The darkness was overwhelming. Even with Moonsnake's torch, they could not see more than a foot in front of them. A crow squawked from overhead. Apart from Crinkle, it was the first sound of life that Andrew had heard since they'd arrived at this strange, decaying place. It was not a comforting sound. It sent a sharp chill down his back, as if it was a warning, urging them to turn back.

'I can't see a thing. How will we know when we've reached the tree?' Andrew said. He stumbled with his arms held out in front of him. Twigs were snapping all around, but there was no reply.

He stopped.

'Poppy?' he said.

No answer.

His voice became more panicked. *'Dan? Moonsnake?'*

Silence.

He was all alone. He began running, shouting.

'Dan, Poppy, Moonsnake! Where are you?' But his voice bounced against the skeletal trees. The branches creaked in the wind as if in mocking laughter. Andrew gulped, swallowing a wave of fear which had crept up into his throat. He continued walking. After a while, his eyes adjusted to the blackness, enough to make out the outline of trees in front of him. They towered over him like giant claws, waiting to snatch him up. Andrew paused, and took a deep breath. His imagination was zooming into overdrive. He needed to stay calm.

'Andrew?' he heard a voice call.

'Poppy!' Andrew screamed, running again.

'Andrew, where are you?' The voice sounded so close, so near, and yet he couldn't see her.

'Where are you guys?' Dan shouted. His voice was like a tiny echo, trapped in a well.

'I'm here,' Andrew said.

'Where?'

Then, from out of the darkness, a glowing light appeared. Andrew squinted, blinded by its intensity.

It was Poppy. She was grinning. Her long blonde hair and pale face were lit up in the glow of her torch.

'Poppy!' Andrew said, relief flooding through him. He frowned. 'Where'd you find that torch?'

'I… I just had it with me.' She shrugged, and then smiled warmly again. 'Andrew, I've found the tree. Come with me.'

'You've found it?'

'Yes. Hurry, over here.' She took his hand and yanked him towards a blackened oak tree, tarred with soot. There was a hole in the bark, like the mouth of a narrow tunnel. She pointed. 'Through there.'

Andrew frowned. 'This doesn't look like the tree that Crinkle spoke of,' he said. 'It doesn't have a door.'

'It's the tree,' Poppy said, gritting her teeth. 'Go inside. Before it's too late.'

Andrew crept closer towards the tree. Then hesitated. 'No, I think we should wait until Dan and Moonsnake show up. We shouldn't go in without them.'

'Just go inside,' Poppy said, sounding impatient now. 'The others are already in there.'

Why was she being so weird? Andrew took a step back. Something was wrong.

'Andrew! Poppy! Where are you?' Dan shouted from somewhere in the distance.

237

Yes. Something was definitely wrong. Why had Poppy lied? Why had she said that Dan was in the tree when he clearly wasn't?

He peered at her closely. 'Poppy, why do you have a mole on your left arm?'

'What? I've always had a mole there.' She nudged him towards the opening in the tree, but Andrew dug his feet into the earth.

'No. You haven't. You've always had one on your right arm. Never on your left.'

'Stop being silly,' she said, 'and come with me.' She jerked his hand impatiently again but Andrew stood firm. He had seen the yellow flash of anger in her eyes. Only for a split second, and then it was gone. But he had seen it.

'Come on, bro,' she said, smiling again.

'You're not my sister,' he said.

Her eyes narrowed into two dark slits. The hole in the tree opened up into a gaping mouth with hundreds of razor-sharp fangs, shaped like sharks' teeth.

'*Arghh!*' Andrew yelled, as it bit down, jaws slamming together like a vice. He spun around, but his sister…or whatever this *thing* was that was pretending to be his sister, stood in his way. She blinked, and her skin began to melt, sliding off her face like hot wax. What remained was a pitted green face and eyes that glowed yellow in the darkness like two flickering balls of fire.

25

Andrew watched in frozen horror, and then jumped back to life.

'You're not real,' he said. 'This is a dream. You're in my imagination. I can make you go away.'

He extended his palms out and shot a ball of green light at the creature. It roared, filling the forest with a deafening cry. The thing disappeared, fading into the night air, blinking out like a light bulb.

Andrew was submerged into darkness again.

'Andrew!' he heard his twin shout. *The real Poppy?* He couldn't be sure. But he hoped with all his soul that it was.

'Poppy, listen to me. Walk towards my voice.'

'I – I can't see you.'

'I know, but just keep walking. You can do it.'

'Andrew?'

Her voice was getting louder. Closer. He saw a ripple in the air. 'Yes, Poppy, keep walking. I can almost see you.' She began to fade into view, as if she was stepping out from another universe. He grabbed her hand. 'You're safe now,' he said.

She threw her arms around him. 'I was stuck in darkness. You came to me. But it wasn't you, Andrew, it was some sort of monster.'

'I know,' Andrew said, brushing Poppy's hair off her clammy forehead. 'The same thing happened to me. We need to find Moonsnake and Dan. This place, it's playing tricks on our minds.'

They wandered deeper into the forest, holding onto each other's arms, calling out for Moonsnake and Dan.

'Andrew? Poppy?' Dan suddenly appeared in front of them, as if he'd stumbled through a seam in the air. 'Man alive, that was scary.' He froze, frowning. Then he backed away. 'Wait. How do I know that you're both, you know, really you?'

'We're twins. We go to Fairoaks. My favourite food is pizza. Andrew's favourite is roast dinner,' Poppy said. 'Happy now? But how do we know that you're really Dan?'

'I'm adopted. I met you both in the Nightmare Factory. I...'

'OK,' Andrew grinned. 'You're you. We're us. Let's find Moonsnake and get out of here.' Just as he'd spoken these words, Moonsnake appeared from behind them, panting hard.

'Where did I put that emergency beetle juice flask?' he said, scrabbling through his bag. 'I'm sure I packed it. Ah, here it is.' He unscrewed the cap and took a big swig. And then another. He burped loudly and looked up, unperturbed. 'What?'

'No point testing him.' Andrew laughed. 'That's definitely the real Moonsnake Bill.'

'We going to find this tree, then?' Moonsnake said. 'Or wait around here and get eaten alive by dream demons.'

'What did you say?'

'Dream demons. They dwell inside people's dreams and nightmares, and can take the form of anything or anyone. Vesuvius must have planted some here to try and catch us out.'

'Right,' Andrew said, feeling an even greater need to start moving again. 'Come on.'

They trekked through the forest for what felt like several hours, when in reality it was probably only minutes.

'How long have we got before Grimble raises the alarm?' Andrew asked.

'Not long,' Dan said, checking his watch. 'About half an hour.'

'Hey, look,' Poppy said, pointing to a tree in a small

circular clearing in the distance. 'That's the tree that Crinkle told us about.'

Andrew felt his heartbeat quicken. *She was right.*

'What are you on about?' Moonsnake said. 'There's two trees there, not one.' He squinted. 'Oh, wait,' he said, hiccupping. 'I'm seeing double again. On we go.'

Poppy shook her head in disapproval.

'Maybe you should lay off the beetle juice,' she said.

They raced over to the tree. Moonsnake staggered in a sort of zigzag. 'No more drink,' Andrew said, taking the flask from him. 'You need to keep a clear head.'

'Too late for that,' Dan muttered, as Moonsnake let out a loud burp.

The tree looked like an open claw, reaching palm-up into the air. Its bark was dead and blackened like the rest of the trees in the forest. A few pitiful brown leaves fell from its branches and fluttered to the ground. There was a small door set in the bark, barely visible to anyone who didn't know it was there.

'Here goes,' Andrew said, and knocked three times on the hollow trunk.

They waited. Nothing happened. Andrew was about to suggest they keep looking, when the earth began to rumble underneath them. Stones and leaves danced on the forest floor like jumping jacks. An icy wind swept all around them, blowing Andrew's hair in his face. Then suddenly, without warning, the roots of the tree erupted from the ground. Andrew and the others were thrown onto their backs. The roots slithered over them like spindly brown fingers, snatching them up and pulling them downwards through the earth.

26

Andrew thrashed about, clawing at the soil. He needed to get back up to the surface. He needed air. He tried to breathe, but his mouth filled with dirt. Earth was all around him, above and below. He tried to kick his feet, but it was no use. His lungs felt tight. His head pounded. Crinkle had *tricked* them. He was sure this was how he was going to die, buried alive with the worms...

He felt himself being pushed down again, drilling through the earth, deeper and deeper underground. Then he felt the roots loosen their grip and his feet were suddenly free, kicking at nothing but air. Then his waist. Then his torso. He fell and landed on something hard. He grumbled, putting a hand to his head.

Was he dead? Had he suffocated? Or was he still alive, stuck in the mud, and this was all just a hallucination, brought on by lack of oxygen?

He sat up. He was in a long white room with a door at one end. Earth was caked on his clothes and in his hair. He probably looked like Stig of the Dump, but he didn't care. *Where were the others?*

Just as this thought crossed his mind, there was a loud thud as Poppy landed on the floor beside him. Then two more thuds as Dan and Moonsnake landed next to her.

Poppy sat up, choking, gasping for air. Andrew thumped her on the back and she spluttered up a mixture of spit and earth. 'Thanks,' she croaked.

'That stupid dwarf,' Dan said. 'I knew we couldn't trust him.'

'What makes you say that?' Moonsnake said, getting up. 'He got us where we wanted to be, didn't he?'

'What? Stuck six feet underground?' Andrew laughed. 'Yeah, fantastic.'

'No, into the next stage of the dream. And look, there's a door, which means there's a way out,' Moonsnake said. 'Come on. Hurry.'

Andrew got to his feet but buckled in pain.

'Andrew, are you OK?' Poppy asked, holding him up.

He looked at her, vision blurring. *Oh no...it was happening again...* His head throbbed. Bile rose in his throat.

'*I am coming for you,*' the voice boomed inside his head.

'Vesuvius. He knows,' Andrew said, dropping to his knees. He could feel Vesuvius's anger racing through his body as if it was his own, filling his veins with a poisonous fury.

'*There will be no running from me this time. I will kill you.*'

What? Andrew thought, paralysed with fear. Vesuvius is travelling to Nusquam? Or was he already here? Andrew sucked in a deep breath, feeling dizzy and faint. The stabbing pain in his head slowly ebbed away.

'Did you have another vision?' Dan said, stepping in front of him. 'Did you see Vesuvius?'

'No.' Andrew shook his head. 'But I heard him and felt him. He was inside my head.'

'Then he's close,' Poppy said. Her hands were trembling inside her pockets. 'Possibly even inside the Dreamsphere. We need to get moving.'

They ran through the doorway into another room, just as bare as the first. No windows. No doors.

'Wait,' Moonsnake said, staring at the floor. 'We're in the same room that we just came from.'

'We can't be,' Andrew said. 'That's impossible.'

'But look,' Moonsnake said. 'There's muddy footprints on the floor from when we fell through the tree. And Poppy's puke. Sorry for pointing that out.'

'No, it's OK,' Poppy said. 'You're right.'

Andrew looked. Moonsnake *was* right. But how could that be?

'Wait a second,' Poppy said, tilting her head as if she'd just had a sudden brainwave. She poked her head through the door again.

'The mud is on the left side in this room, and on the right in the other.'

'So?' Dan said. 'What are you saying?'

'It's a reflection.'

'Huh?'

'Remember what Grimble said to us before we left?'

'No.'

'He said that a lot of things are backwards in the Dreamsphere. Perhaps he was trying to give us a clue.'

'Hmm, a reflection,' Moonsnake said, putting a finger to his lips as if deep in thought. 'Poppy, you received a mirror from my shop, correct?'

'Sure, it's right here,' she said, digging a hand into her pocket and pulling it out. 'Do you think it'll help us get out of here?'

'Well, I could be wrong about this, but yes, I do.

Walk around the room with it. Tell me what you see.'

'Urm, OK,' Poppy said. She moved around the room, holding the mirror up at different angles. 'Just plain white walls.'

'Nothing more?' Moonsnake said. 'Keep trying.'

'But why? What is she looking for?' Andrew said.

Moonsnake didn't answer.

'All I'm getting is walls,' Poppy said. 'Listen, I don't get why I'm…' Her voice trailed off. 'Wait. I see something.'

'You do?' Moonsnake said. 'What do you see?'

'A door. I see a door!'

'What?' Andrew said, running over to her. 'Give that here.' He took the mirror, and stood peering into it with his back to the wall. He could see nothing at first, then a glimpse of a door. He moved the mirror an inch sideways. Yes, it was definitely a door, made from solid dark wood and with a rusty handle.

'Wow,' he said. 'You're right.' He turned around. Just a plain white wall again. 'But that's impossible.'

Moonsnake smiled. 'Nothing's impossible—'

'In the Dreamsphere,' Andrew finished. 'I know. I'm starting to realise that.'

'But how can there be a door in a mirror, when there isn't a door in real life?' Dan complained.

'It's a reflection of an invisible door,' Moonsnake said. 'It's there, you just can't see it.'

Andrew nodded. 'Like Crinkle was reflected in the water,' he said. He stepped back, still holding up the mirror with one hand, and with the other he began to feel around the bare white wall. The wooden doorframe was rough against his fingertips. He gripped the cold metal clasp and turned the doorknob. A crack appeared in the wall behind him.

'Looks like we've found our way out,' he grinned.

He pressed his hand against the wall and the door swung open further. They stepped through it into another room, which was narrow and long. The walls and the ceiling were made from steel, and Andrew could see his grubby face reflected everywhere he looked. At the end of the room was a sheet of vertical blackened glass.

Andrew had expected to face some awful, monstrous-looking beast or something.

'Is this it?' he said.

'Yeah, man,' Dan said. 'I thought it was going to be much harder.'

'What do you think it is? What do we have to do?' Andrew asked.

'Maybe it's a puzzle,' Moonsnake said. 'And once we

solve it, it lets us through to the next section.'

'It seems too easy,' Poppy said, biting her lip. 'We're missing something here. Something to do with the floor.'

'I doubt it,' Andrew said. He stepped forwards onto the first tile. He turned around, grinning. 'See? It's fine. It's just a regular floor.' He stepped onto the second tile, but it crumbled under his foot like polystyrene. Poppy grabbed him by the hood as he dangled above a pit of darkness.

27

Andrew stared down into the abyss. It looked as if it went on for miles, possibly forever. He was hanging over it like a helpless worm on a hook. If Poppy let go, he'd tumble into oblivion.

'Pull me up,' he said. 'Quick!' His heart was pounding, sweat dripping from his brow.

'I can't, you're too heavy. Moonsnake, help me lift him.'

Andrew felt another hand grab his hood and heave him up onto the platform.

'Phew,' Andrew said, still shaking. 'That was close. Thanks, sis.'

'I told you it wasn't *just* a floor,' Poppy said with a knowing grin.

'I know, I know. I should have listened.' He paused. 'So how do we get across, then?'

'Well, I doubt the tiles just drop randomly. You stepped on a purple tile and it didn't fall. Then you stepped on a black one and it did. There must be a pattern,' Poppy said. 'Some kind of rule.'

'Perhaps they go diagonally,' Dan said. 'Hold onto me. I'm going to try one of them out.'

Andrew grabbed Dan's left arm while Moonsnake took hold of his right.

'OK, here goes,' Dan said. 'Are you sure you've got me?'

Andrew and Moonsnake nodded. He stepped onto a bright pink tile diagonal to the dark blue one.

For a moment, nothing happened. Dan let out a sigh of relief. 'Told you,' he said, turning his head. Then the tile shattered and Dan plummeted through the hole. Andrew was nearly tugged down with him but he dug his heels into the ground and held on tight.

'Pull me up! Pull me up now,' Dan shrieked, screwing his eyes shut.

'I – I think your hands are slipping,' Andrew said with a grin.

'Don't even joke about it,' Dan growled.

They heaved him back up to safety. He stumbled backwards, unsteady on his feet. 'Whoa, I'm not trying that again,' Dan said, catching his breath.

'Maybe if we just run really quickly, we'll get to the other side before any of the tiles fall,' Andrew suggested.

'What if some of them fall more quickly than others?' Poppy said. 'No. It's too risky. I'm going to try and figure this out with my brain.' She stepped onto the purple tile and then onto the dark blue tile, and then very tentatively moved diagonally onto a lighter blue square.

Andrew's eyes were fixed on the tile, waiting for it to shatter like the others had. He stood with his hands held out, ready to catch her if she fell. But after thirty seconds, the tile was still in place. 'I'm going to try one more,' Poppy said.

She took a step forward onto a green tile. Andrew quickly moved onto the lighter blue square, just behind her.

They waited. Nothing happened.

'How did you know that it wouldn't fall?' Moonsnake, who was still standing by the door, asked.

'Richard of York gave battle in vain,' Poppy smiled.

'Say what now?' Dan said, looking bemused.

'Red, Orange, Yellow, Green, Blue, Indigo and Violet. The colours of the rainbow. But in this case, they're backwards. If I'm right, which I think I am, the next tile we need to step on should be yellow.' She took a stride forward, missing a white and a luminous green tile in between. Andrew held his breath.

'OK,' Poppy said, letting out a sigh of relief. 'I think I've cracked it.' She leapt onto the orange tile, and then onto the red one, and jumped onto the platform on the other side. 'There, I made it.'

'Well done, mate!' said Dan.

'Yeah, that was awesome,' Andrew said. 'I don't think I could have remembered the colours of the rainbow, let alone backwards.'

'Me neither,' Moonsnake said. They followed Poppy's lead and jumped across to the other side.

The pane of glass gradually lifted upwards, and they were able to walk through into the next section.

'What's this?' Andrew said, as they came to a small table with something carved into the wood. They crowded around. It was a row of strange shapes, like some sort of alien language.

'Maybe it's an ancient Nusquarium language,' Poppy said, looking to Moonsnake Bill for confirmation.

Moonsnake shook his head. 'No, I've never seen anything like this before. I'm not sure what language it is.'

'Maybe it isn't a language at all,' Dan said. 'Maybe it's a code.'

'Do you know,' Poppy said. 'I think that might be the most intelligent thing you've ever said.'

Andrew frowned. 'I'm going to take that as a compliment.'

Poppy twisted her head to look at the shapes. 'It's definitely a code. But it's almost like there's a line that goes straight down the middle. I wonder why...' Her eyes suddenly lit up. 'Andrew, have you still got the mirror?'

'Yeah, here it is.' He passed it to her. 'Why do you want it?'

'I'm going to try something. I think only half of the letters are there. We need a reflection to show us the other half.' She placed the mirror sideways down the centre of the shapes. 'Hmm, nothing that way,' she said. She tried again, this time flipping it around. 'It says something in English,' she said, tilting her head.

'What does it say?' Dan asked, leaning forward eagerly.

'It says...duck.'

'*Duck?*' Andrew said. 'What the hell is *duck* supposed to mean?' He turned around, just as an enormous metal hammer came swinging towards them.

28

Andrew held his hands up, creating a magical defence barrier. The hammer came to a halt just inches away from smashing into their faces.

'Quick. Get down. I can't hold this thing forever.' His voice was strained. He could feel his temples bulging with the pressure. It must have been at least five tonnes of solid metal. Poppy, Dan and Moonsnake dropped to their stomachs. 'Are you sure we're low enough?' Poppy asked.

'Let's hope so,' Andrew said, as he got down on the floor, lying flat on his back. He lowered his arms, releasing the defence barrier and letting the metal hammer swing over them. It smashed through the pane of glass with an ear-splitting crash. They were showered in a storm of broken glass. Andrew glanced down at his arms, which were covered in cuts.

Oh well, he thought. It was better than being knocked out by a giant hammer…

'That was close,' Moonsnake said, grinning.

They hurried over to the metal door. There was

a keyboard of letters and numbers attached to the wall beside it.

'Right,' Poppy said, smiling. 'All we have to do now is work out what the code is to let us in.'

'Easier said than done,' Dan said. 'I'm just wondering what happens if we get it wrong.'

'Hmm, probably best not to think about that,' Moonsnake said. 'Why don't you try "duck"? That could possibly work.'

'Or how about "Vesuvius", backwards?' Andrew said.

'Sounds good to me,' Poppy said.

Andrew typed 'suivusev' into the keyboard. When he'd pressed the last letter, the door began beeping. He turned around, looking at the others. 'Err, is that a good thing?'

'It doesn't appear so,' Moonsnake said, pointing to the walls on either side of them. Andrew gasped, his stomach flipping over. The walls had started moving together, sliding slowly towards them. Soon they'd be flattened to a pulp.

'Great,' Dan said. 'Now what are we gonna do? I don't want to be squashed alive!'

'Don't worry,' Moonsnake said. 'I doubt you'd be alive for very long.'

'Moonsnake,' Andrew growled. 'You're not helping.

How long do you think we've got before they reach us?'

Moonsnake looked at the walls. 'I don't know…ten minutes maybe. Twelve until they squash our brains together like a lemon juicer.'

'He puts it so eloquently,' Dan said, glaring at him. 'Come on. We'd better hurry up and work out what this stupid code is.' He began frantically typing words into the keyboard.

'Stop!' Poppy shouted. 'The walls are speeding up every time you get it wrong.' She yanked him back. 'We can't let ourselves panic. We need to think calmly. Logically.'

'I would,' Dan sneered. 'But it's kinda hard to stay calm when we're about to be made into human mush!'

'OK,' Andrew said, trying to ignore him. 'What clues do we have? Every other time, they've been right under our noses. Look around the place. See if you can find anything.'

They began searching the room for clues. Anything they could use to try and crack the code. For several minutes, they found nothing. Andrew wiped the beads of sweat dripping from his brow. The walls were sliding closer towards them like solid waves of concrete.

'Hey, what's that?' Dan said, pointing to a patch of

wall next to the door. A layer of wallpaper was peeling away, revealing what looked like writing. They got down on their knees, scraping the wallpaper off with their bare hands. Moonsnake was using the blade of his sword.

'What does it say?' Dan said.

Andrew knelt closer, reading the strange inscription.

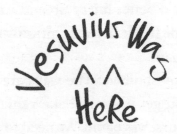

'What good is that to us?' Dan said. He slumped down. 'We've already tried the name Vesuvius, backwards and forwards, and it doesn't work.'

'Look,' Poppy said. 'What are those weird symbols in the middle? They look like cat ears.'

Andrew peered at it again. 'You're right, but what could they mean?'

Poppy took out the mirror and held it up against the inscription, first vertically, and then sideways.

'Look!' she said, squealing with excitement. 'When you hold the mirror horizontally through the centre, "0xx8" appears.'

'I think I love you right now,' Dan said, throwing

his arms around her. He coughed. 'Now hurry up, we don't have long.'

She typed the code into the keyboard and the door beeped again. This time, the red light flashed green. The walls stopped moving, and the door clicked open.

Everyone jumped up and down, elated, screaming. 'Thank god for that,' Andrew said.

They stepped through into the next room. It was full of feathers. There were dreamcatchers hanging from the ceiling, quills, feather pillows, fishing flies, Indian hats, feathered masks. Any object that Andrew could possibly imagine that had feathers on it was right here in this room.

'This isn't going to be easy,' he said, pushing through some of the feathers that lined the floor. 'The Fender's Feather could be any one of these. We have no idea what it looks like.'

'True,' Poppy said, grinning like a Cheshire cat.

'What?' Andrew said. He knew that smug look. It usually meant she knew something that he didn't. He allowed a smile to cross his face. 'What are you thinking?'

Poppy took the dark bulb out of her pocket and held it up. 'Since I got given this, I've been thinking, why? Why would I ever want to be submerged in darkness? I hate the dark. And the only thing I could think of was, what if I wanted to be able to see something that could only be seen with the lights turned off?'

'Right,' Andrew said, 'But I still don't get why that would help us now.'

'Listen, do you remember what Oran said about the Fender bird? He said it used to light up the night sky like a shooting star. Don't you see? It must have glowed in the dark.'

'Oh,' Dan said, eyes widening. 'You're right.'

'Poppy, you're a genius,' Andrew laughed.

'Thanks,' she said. She switched the dark bulb on and the light from the room disappeared like it had been sucked into a vacuum. Andrew stared into the blackness. From somewhere in the corner came a dull glow. He ran over to it, nearly tripping over whatever was strewn across the floor. The light was filtering out of the cracks of a wooden box. He carefully picked it up and opened the lid.

'Wow,' he whispered. Inside was a feather glowing so brightly that Andrew had to shield his eyes from the glare. He put it back in the box.

He looked up, grinning. 'We've found it,' he said. 'We've found the Fender's Feather!'

The door burst open. There was a flash of blinding intensity, and Poppy screamed, collapsing to the ground.

29

'**P**oppy!' Andrew shouted. He ran over to her. Through the darkness, he could just make out the figure of a boy standing in the doorway.

There was a wicked laugh.

'Jason?'

'Yep. That's right,' Jason said, still laughing. He held Oran's unicorn horn in the air and the room filled with an eerie purple light.

'How did you get here before Vesuvius?' Andrew said, eyes narrowing, expecting him to come crashing through the door at any second.

Jason pushed his shoulders back, seeming to grow a little taller. 'I followed you here. And now I'm going to prove once and for all that I am more powerful than you are.'

'Shur're scum,' Poppy spat. Her lip was swollen and bleeding from smacking it against the floor. 'Shou'll never be as powerful as my brother. He's the Weleaser. Shou're just…Wesuvius's little punk.'

'Shut up,' Jason said, red with anger. He pointed the

unicorn horn at her again, ready to finish her off.

'Wait,' Andrew said. 'Don't do that. She's helpless. I'm the one who you want. So let us finish this between us. Just you and me.'

Jason lowered the unicorn horn in hesitation, but only slightly.

'Look, you'd be proving nothing by killing my twin. And you don't want to be known for killing an unarmed, feeble little girl, do you?'

Poppy glared up at Andrew, but he didn't care. Jason wouldn't be able to kill her now. He wouldn't want Andrew to think he was gutless.

'OK,' Jason said. 'I won't kill her…' He paused, smirking, then added, 'Yet.' He pointed the unicorn horn at Andrew. 'Besides, I'd like her to watch as I squash you like a bug.'

Poppy growled again and scrambled to her feet. Her legs gave way and she collapsed to the ground.

'Poppy, stay out of this,' Andrew yelled. 'All of you, keep back. This is between me and Jason.' He stepped forward, but before he did something that he might regret, he wanted to try and reason with Jason. 'Look, why are you doing this? You're a jerk, yes.' Jason clenched his fist around the unicorn horn like he was about to use it. 'But you're not evil. Vesuvius has got inside your brain. He's warped your entire way of thinking. You're not a killer. You know you're not a killer.'

Jason smirked. 'I killed your friend Oran, didn't I?' He laughed again. 'Oh, but you wouldn't know that, would you? Because as he was dying, you were running away like a coward.'

A thorn of anger pierced Andrew's chest. Or was it guilt? He ground his teeth together, trying to remain calm. 'Look, Jason, I don't want to kill you, but if I have to, I will.'

Jason licked his lips. 'Not if I kill you first.' There was a blast of bright purple light. Andrew put his hands up, moulding the air around him into a defence barrier. The light bounced off like rain beating against a windowpane, then hit the floor.

Jason's cheek twitched irritably. He raised the unicorn horn again, but before he could use it, the door flew open and Madam Bray appeared.

Jason twisted around. 'What are you doing here?'

'Stopping you,' she said, and then lifted something black and square up to his neck. Jason shook as if he was being electrocuted, and then with a look of frozen horror he dropped to the floor.

30

Andrew stood very still, too stunned to move. Too confused to speak. Was Madam Bray protecting him? Was she on their side now? It didn't make any sense.

'Oh, don't look so surprised.' Madam Bray sneered. 'I didn't do it for you. I did it for him. For his own good.'

'Huh?' Dan said. 'You killed him. He's dead…isn't he?'

'No. I merely stunned him with this.' She held up some sort of Taser. 'All I can say is thank you for not harming him before I got here. Because we all know who would have won that fight.' She looked at Andrew with a poignant stare.

'What?' Andrew said. He really didn't get what was going on. 'You were protecting Jason? But…*why*?'

'He's my nephew,' Madam Bray said. She sighed, as if she was utterly exhausted. She had big dark circles under her eyes. Her cheeks were sunken and pale. 'When I got back from the Nightmare Factory, I went to live with Jason and my sister. I came to realise how much I'd missed out on life. I hadn't seen my sister, Carry, Jason's mother, since I'd been stolen from my dreams as a child. I'd never even met my own nephew, for goodness sake.' She laughed dryly. 'My hatred for Vesuvius returned, stronger than ever, and I ignored his constant calls inside my dreams, asking for help to release him. As far as I was concerned, I wanted nothing more to do with him.'

'So…what happened?' Andrew said, taking a deep breath. He couldn't believe what she was saying. All this time he had thought she had been the spy, when it had been Jason all along.

'Vesuvius began contacting Jason through his dreams instead. I wanted him to stay away from you at school. I didn't want him getting mixed up with it all. Little did I know he already was.' A single tear rolled down her cheek.

Andrew swallowed. He'd never seen Madam Bray cry before. He'd never even imagined that she was capable of such emotions. But then it dawned on him: she was just like them. Stolen from her dreams as a child, she'd had her life completely turned upside down by Vesuvius. He almost felt sorry for her.

'It's OK,' Andrew said. 'Tonight, we're going to end

this. We have the Fender's Feather now. All we need to do is get back to the dream factory and…'

'No,' Madam Bray said, shaking her head. 'Vesuvius won't let you. He'll be waiting.'

'Do you know where?' Moonsnake asked.

'Not a clue. In the Dreamsphere, maybe. In Nusquam. Who knows? But he's not going to let you walk away alive.'

Andrew swallowed, remembering Tiffany's prophecy. *One of you will die…* He felt his body turn weak. 'We told Jason about the prophecy, so Vesuvius must know about it too.'

Dan put his head in his hands. 'Great, so he knows everything. Can you tap into his thoughts again? See where he is?'

'I'll try,' Andrew said. He sat down on the floor. He shut his eyes, concentrating hard on Vesuvius. His head flashed with an angry pain, as sharp as daggers.

I'm waiting for you.

He was engulfed by a sudden blackness.

'He's blanking me out,' Andrew said. 'He knows that I'm trying to read his mind. But you're right – he's after us.' Andrew cradled the box with the Fender's Feather inside, holding it tight.

'You shouldn't keep it in there,' Madam Bray said.

'It'll be easier for Vesuvius to steal back like that.'

'Never thought I'd say this, mate, but she's right. You need to ditch the box and hide that thing,' said Dan.

'OK,' Andrew said. He opened up the lid and took out the glowing green feather. 'Whoa,' he said, as bright light filled the room.

'What's happening?' Moonsnake asked, peering around.

The walls were melting, blurring into a misty rainbow of colours, like spilled petrol. Then the mist began to clear slowly, and they were left in a dark room with thousands of dazzling stars floating in the night sky.

Wait. They're not stars, they're dreams, Andrew thought. He was lying on the pier in the centre of the Dreamsphere, looking up. He shot to his feet, fear punching his chest.

Vesuvius! Where was he? But there was no sign of him. He sighed with relief. They'd beaten him to it.

Poppy was slumped beside him. She half stirred. 'Where are we?' she whispered, before closing her eyes again.

'Moonsnake, I want you to take Poppy back to your house, OK? She's not well. She needs a healing potion.

Meet us back at the Dream Factory in a few hours.'

Moonsnake nodded. 'Of course.' He picked Poppy up and draped her over his shoulder.

Madam Bray and Jason were over by the door. Jason was curled up on the floor in a ball, unconscious.

'Come on, let's get going,' Andrew said to Dan. 'We need to get this back to the Dream factory.' He slipped the feather inside his boot and walked down the pier. He reached for the door handle.

A green blistering light shot out at him. Andrew was thrown backwards. He hit the deck with a thud, rolling several times. He grabbed the edge, stopping himself from falling off. His mind was spinning. His vision blurred. But in front of him, in the light of the doorway, he could just make out the blackened figure of Vesuvius.

31

Andrew jumped to his feet. Vesuvius stood facing him, his cruel dark eyes fierce with anger. Grimble was by his side, holding the keys to the Dreamsphere with a trembling hand.

'Give me the feather, Andrew,' Vesuvius hissed, stepping towards him, 'and nobody needs to get hurt.'

'Yeah, right,' Andrew said, and he raised his palms, sending a wave of light at him. Vesuvius lifted a hand and created a defence barrier, as if he was doing nothing more than swatting a fly. He shot a flare of light back and Andrew clutched his right shoulder as it struck him, yelling in pain.

Vesuvius laughed. 'I have grown more powerful since the last time we met, Andrew. You should know that by now.'

He raised his cane and Andrew felt himself being picked up off the floor, held in the air like a beetle in amber. He tried to kick his legs, thrash his arms, but he couldn't fight the energy that was keeping him locked there. Vesuvius flicked his wrist and sent Andrew flying backwards, smacking into the concrete wall behind him. Pain ripped through every muscle in his body. Any normal person would have died instantly, but Andrew still had the ability to heal himself. He shut his eyes, feeling a warm glow radiate through his entire body, heating up his insides as if he was being wrapped up in an electric blanket.

Every inch of his body twanged with exhaustion. He didn't have enough energy left to fight.

'Give me the feather,' Vesuvius said again.

Andrew opened his mouth, managing to muster a couple of words. 'No. Never.'

'Fine. Have it your way,' Vesuvius spat. He strode towards him.

'*Oi!* Vesuvius!' Dan yelled, running up from behind him. He plunged a glow knife into his back.

Vesuvius spun around, eyes blazing. 'Get out of my way,' he shouted, pointing his cane at Dan and firing a shard of dazzling light at him.

Dan collapsed to the floor, but Andrew could see his chest moving slightly. He was still alive!

Vesuvius growled and pulled the knife out of his back. Andrew spotted Moonsnake and Poppy creeping towards the door, and he took this opportunity to blast Vesuvius, catching him off guard. The streams of light hit Vesuvius straight in the chest. There was an ear-piercing yell of fury. Vesuvius straightened up, flexing his back. He spun back around, grinning like a hyena.

What was wrong? Why wasn't it affecting him? Andrew glanced at the door. Moonsnake Bill and Poppy were gone. At least they had managed to escape…

'You will pay for that,' Vesuvius said. He lifted his skull cane in the air.

In the corner of his vision, Andrew could see Grimble also sneaking towards the door.

'Where do you think you're going?' Vesuvius hissed, his head snapping around to face him. 'You let the boy inside the Dreamsphere and now he has the feather. It's your fault this has happened.' He wrapped his bony fingers tightly around the skull cane, and pointed it at Grimble.

Grimble froze, terror in his eyes. 'But, sire, I did all you asked of me. Please, have mercy—'

'Mercy? I'll show you mercy.' He pointed the skull cane at Grimble and a green light shot out of the end, sending him flying through the air.

Thud.

He hit the wall beside Andrew. There was the unmistakeable sound of fracturing bones. Andrew turned to look at him. Grimble was lying haphazardly on the floor, neck twisted at a sharp ninety degree angle.

'For what you did, you're lucky I didn't drag it out further. Believe me, Grimble, if I had the time I would have.' Vesuvius turned, eyes set on Madam Bray. 'And now to deal with you.'

Madam Bray quivered with fear as Vesuvius walked slowly towards her. She grabbed Oran's unicorn horn, and the two began to battle it out.

Grimble's eyes met Andrew's. Two pools of despair, but there was also acceptance in them, an acceptance that Andrew had only ever seen once before – in Oran's eyes. Before he had died.

Barely moving his lips, he whispered something to Andrew.

'The secret of the Dreamsphere is…'

'I can't hear you,' Andrew said, shuffling closer. 'Speak up.'

'You must…fight the darkness and…use the light.'

'What?' Andrew said. He'd heard him clearly this

time. It just didn't make any sense. 'I don't understand. What darkness? What light?'

Grimble reached into his pocket. He pulled out a small remote control, trying his best to conceal it within his sleeve.

He pointed it at the computer and pressed a button. 'Fight the darkness. Use the light,' he said, letting out one final splutter.

'Grimble?' Andrew said. 'Grimble, what does that mean?' But Grimble was no longer breathing. His cold, dead eyes stared through Andrew, unblinking.

Andrew turned. Madam Bray was limping out of the door, her leg shredded as if it'd been used as a dog's chew toy. Jason was slumped over her shoulder, out for the count.

'It's just you and me now, Andrew,' Vesuvius said. He stood on the pier, cackling like a madman. 'And only one of us can survive.'

Andrew dragged himself up. His body ached. His limbs felt weak. He was in no state to fight. But he didn't have a choice.

He would not die weak.

He put his hands in the air, yelling, 'OK, Vesuvius. I'm ready for you. Give me all that you've got.' Just as these words escaped his mouth, all of the stars in the

Dreamsphere began to blink out, and the last thing Andrew saw was Vesuvius's thin, twisted smile, before he was pulled into total darkness.

32

Darkness was all around him, above and below. And then, from within the darkness, a small light floated down towards him. As it got closer, it filled the Dreamsphere with an eerie glow and then exploded like a star.

For a long moment, Andrew was blinded, unable to see anything but colourful dots.

When his vision returned, a sense of dread spread up his body like wildfire. Andrew was back in London. Buildings were burning, completely destroyed. The sky had turned black with thick smoke. Shadowmares spilled out from the darkness, floating towards him. He peered up at the thousands of hungry red eyes and terror seized him. This was his nightmare, and it was all coming true. This time, there was no waking up.

Fear crept through his veins. His muscles locked together. He tried to move but it was as if he was being pinned to the ground by an invisible force. Vesuvius stood over him, laughing wickedly. 'Get used to it, Andrew. I rule the world now.'

Andrew swallowed, unable to breathe. The Shadowmares were almost upon him, their arms outstretched like sleepwalkers. He was engulfed in unbearable cold. He fought to stay conscious, urging himself to think straight, trying to remember how he'd ended up here. Everything was so…hazy. *Where had he been? What had he been doing?* He was sure it was something important, but he couldn't remember what. Nothing was making sense.

The Shadowmares drew breath, sucking all of Andrew's energy from his body, and releasing it in an icy plume of bitter air.

Have to stay awake, Andrew thought. *Need to remember why I'm here.*

A vision of a feather flashed through his mind, as if it was a distant memory, lost deep within his thoughts. Of course… He had been in the Dreamsphere.

He was *still* in the Dreamsphere.

Which meant none of this was real. It was only a nightmare. *His* nightmare.

Vesuvius bent down, and pulled the feather from Andrew's boot. Andrew couldn't stop him. He was so frozen with fear that he couldn't do anything but watch.

'No,' he said, gripped by horror as Vesuvius smiled

and slipped the feather inside his cloak.

Vesuvius pointed his skull cane at Andrew. 'Goodbye, Releaser,' he said.

'If you kill me, you won't be able to stay on Earth. Everything will turn back to normal anyway.' Andrew said.

Vesuvius snarled. 'I have enough of your fear to last me three hundred years or more. By then, I will have found myself a new Releaser.' He raised the cane, and the skull's eyes began to turn red.

Wait. This couldn't be it. This couldn't be how it ended. Andrew racked his brains, trying to think of a way out. Grimble's words rang in his ears like the echo of a bell.

'Fight the darkness. Use the light.'

Andrew knew what he had to do. He had to fight his fear. Fight the darkness inside him. If he let it beat him, Vesuvius would win. He shut his eyes and tried to think happy thoughts. He imagined watching TV with Poppy and Mum, safe in the comfort of his own home. He thought of Dan, and how he couldn't wait to play football with him at school again. He thought about all the people escaping the Fear Farms and being reunited with their families. *Happy, happy thoughts.*

He opened one eye. Yes! It was working. The buildings behind Vesuvius were slowly re-forming. The black smoke was clearing from the sky. Andrew sat up, his muscles springing back to life.

'What are you doing?' Vesuvius hissed. 'You're supposed to be afraid. This is the end of everything. This is Tiffany's prophecy. It's all coming true.' He raised his hands to the sky. 'This is the future.'

'No,' Andrew said, shaking his head. 'It's not.'

He reached into his pocket and took out the ball of light that Moonsnake had given him. It floated above his palm, sparkling like a crystal ball. If he was right, then this globe of light contained Vesuvius's biggest nightmare. This ball of light was *his* ticket out of here. He threw it in the air, and the ball exploded, showering them in glittering sparks.

Andrew felt the dread disappear like a huge weight lifting from his shoulders.

The black sky was bleached of its darkness, gradually turning blue. The smouldering black buildings began returning to normal, the Shadowmares fading into nothing.

'No,' Vesuvius said, as he collapsed to the ground. 'No! This can't be happening. This is the future. This is how the world ends.'

Andrew shook his head. 'Sorry,' he said. 'But you're wrong, Vesuvius. This is the way *you* end.' He bent down and reached into Vesuvius's cloak, taking the feather back.

'No,' Vesuvius said again. His face was filled with rage. His fingers twitched as if he wanted to move his arms, but couldn't find the strength.

Andrew raised his palms. Vesuvius tried to struggle free, but he appeared to be pinned to the ground. Frozen with fear just like Andrew had been. Andrew shot an unending stream of hot green light out of his hands, brighter than he'd ever managed to create before. Vesuvius's tortured screams filled the air as sharp and as deafening as an untuned violin. His veins bulged from his pale skin like cracked blue paint. The light continued to pulse from his fingertips in a spray of dazzling green. After a while, the air grew eerily silent.

Andrew stopped, and peered cautiously at the blackened spot where Vesuvius had been lying. A rush of exhilaration washed through him. Had he really done it? Had he defeated Vesuvius for the final time? He stared at the pile of ash, and swirling black smoke. He had trapped Vesuvius in his own nightmare. He didn't have a soul-catcher, but he didn't need one.

There was no way out of this nightmare for Vesuvius, not anymore.

It was over.

He turned. Where did he go now? How did he get out of this place? Maybe he would be stuck here forever too, but if that was the price to pay for saving the world from destruction, then so be it…

There was a soft glow from up ahead. Andrew squinted. It looked like Oran, but he couldn't be sure. He started running. As he got closer, Oran's smile was unmistakeable. A warm yellow shine was radiating from his body. His skin was almost translucent as if he was a mirage in the middle of the desert.

'Oran,' Andrew said. He wanted to reach out and hug him, but he didn't know if he could. He didn't want to shatter the illusion. 'I'm sorry,' he said. 'We should have stayed behind. We could have saved you.'

'No.' Oran smiled. 'It was how it was supposed to be. You need to leave now. It's time to go back.'

'How?'

'You're still inside Vesuvius's nightmare,' Oran smiled. 'Close your eyes and wake up.' With that, Oran began to fade.

'Wait,' Andrew said, putting his hands out. He had so many things to say. So many things to ask him.

'Another time. Another place,' Oran said with a smile, and he disappeared.

Andrew stood sobbing. Had that been real? Or was it just the Dreamsphere playing tricks on his mind? There was only one way to find out. He shut his eyes. *Wake up*, he thought.

His eyes shot open and he was back on the pier. Dan raced over to him.

'Andrew,' Dan said. 'Are you OK?'

Andrew nodded. But then he frowned.

'What about you? Vesuvius…he hurt you.'

'I'll live,' Dan said. He grinned. 'You did it man, you actually did it. You defeated Vesuvius!'

'It's not over yet,' Andrew said. 'We still need to get this feather to the Dream Factory. Come on. Let's get out of here.'

They hurried down the pier towards the door, where Grimble's body was still slumped against the wall. Andrew paused, filled with a mixture of sadness and admiration.

'Thank you,' he said, peering down at him. 'I guess you were a hero after all.'

33

They travelled back down the long, dark corridor. When they reached the end, Andrew pulled open the door to the dreaming lounge. The light was blinding. The guards were still standing outside.

'Hey,' one of them said, raising his eyebrows. 'Who's with you? Where's Vesuvius?'

'Vesuvius is dead,' Andrew said. 'I killed him.'

The guard with the moustache turned to the other, uncertain. 'What if he's lying? Vesuvius would kill us if we let him past.'

'I'm not lying,' Andrew said. 'If you'd like, I could demonstrate what I did to him on you?' He raised his palms.

The guards' eyes widened. 'No,' the taller one said. 'No, it's alright. You can pass.' They stepped aside.

'Thank you,' Andrew said. 'And by the way, Grimble, your boss, he's in there too. Vesuvius killed him. Make sure you give him a proper burial. I know he probably wasn't the nicest fella, but he saved my life.'

The guards nodded quickly. 'Of course.'

'Good,' Andrew said, and he turned, walking past the empty beds, no longer inhabited by Nusquarium dreamers.

'Do you think the Nusquarium people will be glad that Vesuvius is dead?' Dan asked.

'I should think so, but I reckon the people back home are going to be even gladder.'

They hurried along the dark corridor and outside into the alleyway. Night was falling upon Nusquam like a black veil, and the streets were quiet and eerie as Andrew and Dan began their long trek back to the Dream Factory.

They arrived hours later, feet aching and covered in blisters. The sight of the Dream Factory towering into the sky sent ripples of hope through Andrew. He stumbled up to the door and knocked tiredly.

The door burst open, and Tarker was standing behind it, as if he'd been waiting there the entire time.

'Come in, come in,' he said, ushering them inside.

'Andrew!' Poppy shouted, jumping up from one of the chairs and rushing over. She wrapped her arms around him. 'I knew you'd do it. I knew you'd come back.' She paused. 'Do you have the feather?'

Andrew nodded.

There was a shared sigh of relief between all of them.

'Good,' Moonsnake said, beaming widely. 'Well done.'

'Thanks,' Andrew said. 'I'm so glad you're OK, Poppy. How did you get past the guards outside the Dreamsphere?'

Moonsnake laughed. 'Invisibility potion. Thankfully we had just enough left over.'

Andrew grinned. 'Good thinking.'

'Come,' Tarker said. 'We must place the feather in the central dreamcatcher immediately.'

They followed Tarker through the golden corridors, drenched in warm light from the chandeliers that hung overhead.

They passed the spiralling glass staircase, continuing through the corridor until they reached the Dream-bottling room. It was full of heavy-looking machinery and conveyer belts with vials full of colourful dreams on them. The Luguarna people were scurrying around inspecting the tiny glass vials.

'There's so many of you,' Poppy said. Three months ago, Vesuvius had broken into the Dream Factory and killed most of the Luguarna people. 'They re-populated quickly.'

Tarker nodded.

'Yes. They needed to. Lots of dreams to be made,' he said.

He opened a door that led down another, much narrower corridor. Tarker stopped at a room with a sign hanging on the door saying 'Private. No entry'.

He fumbled around with the keys for a moment until he found a small golden one that slotted into the lock. The door swung open. Inside was a dusty white room with no windows.

Poppy sneezed. 'When was the last time somebody cleaned this place?' she said, eyes watering.

'A while ago.' Tarker hobbled over to a large object in the corner of the room, covered by a sheet with about three years' worth of dust on it. He wheeled the object out and pulled the sheet off. 'I give you the central dreamcatcher.'

A breath caught in Andrew's throat. 'Wow,' he said.

Moonsnake Bill took a swig from his flask and scratched his head in disbelief. 'Well I never.'

It looked like a big generator with two metal prongs sticking out of it. Between the prongs was a huge wicker dreamcatcher, minus the feathers. Andrew had never seen anything like it before.

'So…err, this is what's going to save the world?' Dan said dubiously.

Tarker nodded. 'Oran invented it years ago, when he first found out about the feather, before he began believing that it was just a myth.'

'Does it actually work?' Andrew asked.

'After everything we've just gone through, I'd say let's hope so,' Dan said.

'No way to know until we try,' Tarker said. 'Pass me the feather.'

Andrew reached into his boot and pulled out the Fender's Feather. He handed it to Tarker, who tied a piece of string onto the end of it and attached it to the giant dreamcatcher.

Andrew waited, holding his breath.

'Why isn't anything happening?'

Tarker opened his fist, and revealed a small remote control in the palm of his hand. He pointed it at the device and pressed a button.

The generator groaned like a computer starting up. Several seconds later, a brilliant blue light travelled up the prongs, crackling and buzzing as it reached the top. The dreamcatcher lit up as if a mini storm was raging inside it. The electricity illuminated every part of the web.

'Amazing,' Andrew muttered, shaking his head. 'Absolutely unreal.' Eventually the blue light stabilised, leaving the dreamcatcher glowing softly.

'So what now?' Poppy asked.

Andrew smiled. 'Now? Now we go back and see if it worked.'

34

Andrew turned to Moonsnake Bill, and after a short pause, threw his arms around him. The sweet smell of beetle juice and leather drifted up his nose. He'd known Moonsnake Bill for less than two days, but he had a feeling he was going to miss him.

'Thank you for everything. We couldn't have done it without you,' he said, pulling back.

Moonsnake Bill waved a hand. 'It was nothing, just another adventure. Don't be a stranger now. Come and visit whenever you like.'

'We will,' Poppy said, giving him a hug. She glanced away. 'Sorry that I thought you were a bit of a nutcase when I first met you.'

Moonsnake Bill chuckled loudly. 'That's OK. It wouldn't be the first time.'

Dan slapped him on the back. 'Good meeting you Moonsnake. We'll catch you soon.'

Moonsnake Bill nodded, smiling sadly. 'That you will. Have a safe journey back.' He turned to Tarker. 'So, do I get a guided tour of the Dream Factory then?'

They walked off down the corridor together.

'We'd better leave,' Andrew said to the others. 'We still need to find out if the feather worked.'

They hurried back to Oran's dining room.

'Stand on the rug,' Andrew told them. 'And shut your eyes.'

'Where are we going?' Poppy asked.

'I don't know; somewhere that we can check everything's back to how it should be. Piccadilly Circus?'

Dan and Poppy nodded. 'OK.'

Andrew closed his eyes. 'Aska Babaka, Nusquam arrow. Take us to where we want to go.'

They were thrust into the tunnel of light and darkness once more, zooming through it as if they were catapulting through some sort of wormhole. Andrew relaxed this time, concentrating on where he wanted to go. 'Piccadilly Circus. Piccadilly Circus,' he said, over and over again.

He landed firmly on his feet outside Piccadilly Circus tube station.

'Wow,' he said to himself. 'I'm really starting to get the hang of this teleportation business.'

Poppy and Dan landed next to him, tumbling along the pavement until they finally rolled to a stop. Poppy got up, yanking up her socks and smoothing her hair.

Andrew gazed at the street. The buildings were burnt, cars were upturned like toys, shop windows were smashed, but something was different. There were no monsters anywhere. People lingered in groups, working together to pick up rubbish and glass. They were smiling, no longer consumed by fear.

A man in overalls stood on a ladder painting over the 'Fear Farm' sign with white paint. Andrew wandered up to him.

'Excuse me,' he said. 'What's happened to all the people that were being kept down there?'

The man turned, beaming at him. 'Haven't you heard? They've all been freed. The council has set up rescue centres because the hospitals are all full. I think the nearest one is just down the road.' He pointed towards a street. 'Down there and turn left.'

'Thank you,' Andrew said. 'Over here,' he shouted to Andrew and Poppy.

They raced past the fountain and down the road until they came to a large building with a sign outside saying 'Piccadilly Treatment Centre'. They ran up the steps and knocked on the door.

A woman in a blue nurse's outfit appeared from inside. 'Hello,' she said. 'What can I do for you? Are you hurt?'

'No, we're fine,' Poppy said. 'But we think our mum might be in here, and someone else we know too.'

The woman reached behind the door and pulled out a clipboard. 'Names?'

'Ours or theirs?' Dan said.

The woman looked up, raising an eyebrow.

'Cynthia Lake and Tiffany Grey,' Andrew said. 'Are they here?'

The woman ran her finger down the list. 'Doesn't look like it, sorry.'

Andrew felt his heart plummet. 'Well they must be around here somewhere. Tiffany was snatched not far from here and my mum lives nearby too.'

'You might want to try the unit just down the road. That white building over there. The old Fitness Fanatics gym.' She pointed to a blue building on the other end of the street.

'Thanks,' Andrew said. He turned to Poppy and Dan. 'Come on.' They sprinted down the street until they reached a building which had a sign saying 'Fitness Fanatics' on it and then a smaller sign below it reading 'Treatment Centre.' They wandered inside.

A nurse with a bun stepped in front of them.

'Who are you here to see?' she asked.

'My mum,' Andrew said. 'Cynthia Lake.'

'And our friend Tiffany Grey,' Dan added.

The nurse nodded. 'Yes, they're here. They've been waiting for you.' She smiled, pulling the door open for them. 'Come in.'

Andrew sighed, relieved. *Finally*, he thought and stepped inside. All the gym equipment had been cleared away, and beds had been lined up against the walls exactly like a hospital. Andrew spotted his mum and Tiffany at opposite sides of the room to each other.

'I'll go and say hi to Tiffany,' Dan said. 'You two go and see your mum.'

'OK,' Andrew said. 'Thanks.'

Poppy and Andrew hurried over to the bed where their mum lay. She was propped up against two big pillows, and had a drip attached to her wrist. Her eyes were big and puffy with dark circles around them, and she looked pale and gaunt – a shadow of her former self.

She beamed when she saw them, reaching out to hug them.

'Mum!' Andrew said, flying into her arms. 'Are you alright?' Poppy came and hugged her too.

Mum kissed them both on the forehead, erupting into tears.

'I thought you were both dead. I thought I'd lost you. I thought—'

'Shh, we're fine, Mum,' Poppy said, burrowing her head into her chest. 'We're all together now.'

'But how did you manage to stay safe for so long? How did you—'

'We hid,' Andrew said. 'In the restaurant that you used to take us to as kids.' He'd tell her the truth one day, but now wasn't the time. 'How are you feeling?' he asked.

'I'm OK,' she sniffed. 'I'm just getting my strength back. They barely fed us while we were locked in those awful contraptions. This whole thing just seems so unreal, doesn't it? Like it's been one enormous nightmare.'

'I know what you mean,' Andrew said. 'So what's this?' he said, pointing to the drip.

'Just to hydrate me, dear.' She smiled. 'Doctor says I should be able to go home tomorrow.'

'Thank God for that,' Poppy said, wiping a tear from her eye.

'They still don't know what happened. Those strange creatures made from the shadows, they've all disappeared now. I hope they never come back.'

Andrew smiled. 'Believe me, they won't.'

His mum frowned. 'Do you know that woman over there? She's waving at you.' Andrew turned, and saw Tiffany sitting up in bed, grinning and beckoning them over.

'Yeah, that's Dan's…err, aunt,' Poppy said. 'She looked after us for a while. We'd better go and say hi. We'll come back in a bit.' They hurried across the room.

'Well done,' Tiffany said, holding her arms out wide and hugging Andrew and Poppy. 'You did it. You saved the world.'

'Yeah,' Andrew said, blushing. 'Yeah, I guess we did.' He looked down, a pang of guilt zapping his stomach. 'But Oran…he's…'

'Dead,' Tiffany said, nodding. 'I know. I always knew.'

'What do you mean?' Poppy said. 'How?'

'Grab a chair and sit down,' Tiffany said with a frown. 'I have something to show you.'

They pulled out three visitors' chairs and placed them around Tiffany's bed.

'So,' Andrew said. 'What is it?'

Tiffany sighed. 'Pass me that leather satchel next to the nightstand,' she said, coughing.

Andrew bent down and lifted the bag up onto her

bed. It weighed a ton. 'Whatever's in this thing, *rocks*?'

Tiffany shook her head, laughing, and pulled out a large green book. Andrew stepped back. Wait – he'd seen this book before. It was the book that contained Tiffany's prophecy. He flicked through to the chapter on Vesuvius. There was a page torn out from the back.

'I'm afraid we didn't tell you the whole truth,' she said with a sigh.

'What do you mean?' Andrew said, raising an eyebrow.

She passed him a loose page, torn at the edges. 'I ripped this out a while ago to protect you, and so that Jason didn't see it.'

Andrew took the page, hands shaking as he read the words.

Boy will arrive and act as false prophet. Oran will die. Andrew will travel to the Dreamsphere and trap Vesuvius in his own nightmare. Fender's Feather will cure the world of fear.

A surge of anger spread through him.

'Tiffany, what is this?'

Tiffany bit her bottom lip. 'After we defeated Vesuvius the first time, I had another dream,' she said. 'The same dream as before, but this time much clearer. I saw two possible futures for the world. One where it was destroyed, and one where it remained as normal. What I didn't realise the first time was that these were not futures at all, but dreams within dreams. They were your nightmare and Vesuvius's. Complete opposites of each other. I was being shown a glimpse of your time in the Dreamsphere, Andrew. I saw you defeating Vesuvius. I also saw the path in which you had to take to arrive at this outcome.'

'Then why didn't you tell me?' Andrew said. 'We could have prevented Oran dying. We could have foreseen Jason betraying us. We could have—'

Tiffany shook her head. Her eyes were misted over with sadness, with pity. 'No,' she said. 'There was no other way. You had to follow the path that was written for you. Or Vesuvius would have won.'

'So… Oran had to die?' Andrew said, trying to understand. 'He didn't have a choice?'

'He had a choice,' Tiffany said. 'I told him about my prophecy, and he made the decision that when the time came, he would go willingly.'

Andrew slumped back in his chair. He wasn't sure if he felt angry about the fact that she'd kept this from him, or sad that it had been the only way to defeat Vesuvius. He felt numb. No wonder Tiffany had given

Jason such a funny look when she had met him. She had known he would be the one to kill Oran.

'But you let us tell him everything. You even showed him the book,' Andrew said.

Tiffany nodded sadly. 'It was the only way. Believe me, if there was another path we could have taken…a way to save Oran, I would have done it.' She blinked back tears.

'Well, I never would have befriended that creep Jason if I'd known,' Dan said with gritted teeth. He turned to Andrew and Poppy. 'Do you think he'll come back to Fairoaks?'

'Madam Bray I can deal with,' Andrew said. 'But if Jason comes back, well, I might not be able to hold my tongue.'

'Try to remember,' Tiffany said, 'that Jason was not in his right mind when he did all of those things. I'm not saying you have to like him, but at least try to understand, it was Vesuvius that was filling his head with such thoughts.'

'I suppose so,' Andrew said. 'I still think he's a nasty creep though.'

'Me too,' Poppy said.

'I wish we'd had a chance to say goodbye to Oran,' Dan said, looking at the floor.

'I know,' Tiffany said. 'We did consider telling you, but we couldn't risk the chance of Vesuvius discovering the *real* truth about the Prophecy.' She paused. 'Oran was honoured to die for such a cause. We must remember that.'

Andrew nodded, swallowing back tears. 'You're right.' He took a deep breath. 'Come on, we'd better go and help clean up outside. There's so much to do to get this place back to normal.'

'Agreed,' Poppy said. 'And I want to go and find the kids I was looking after, make sure they're all OK.'

They said goodbye to Tiffany and their mum, and headed outside into the cool, fresh air. They picked up brooms and began sweeping glass off the streets.

'Do you think Vesuvius will ever find a way out of the Dreamsphere?' Poppy asked.

Andrew paused, thinking about this for a moment. Then: 'I really don't know,' he said honestly. 'I don't think so. But it's like Oran once said, "You can't change life. What will happen, will happen. You just have to face your fear and jump in for the ride".'

And that's exactly what he intended to do.

About the Author

L ucy Jones is twenty-five years old but has been writing stories since she was twelve. *The Nightmare Factory* was her first novel. She is fascinated by all things supernatural, and has a huge passion for reptiles, especially snakes. In her spare time she enjoys watching horror films and going to rock festivals. She currently lives in Exmouth, Devon, with her dog, Boo.

www.lucyjonesbooks.co.uk

Acknowledgments

A huge thank you to everyone who helped with the publication of *Rise Of The Shadowmares*, and in particular to my agent Madeleine Milburn and my editor, Matt Ralphs. Rebecca Hearne, for helping me with promotion, and for all her guidance. Mark Stuart and Sarah Moass – AKA 'Vesuvius' and 'Tiffany Grey'. The South West SCBWI group – for all their support and encouragement.

My parents, for always being there.

ANTHONY
HOROWITZ

ANTHONY
HOROWITZ
TWIST COTTAGE
ACCIDENTS WILL HAPPEN...

ANTHONY
HOROWITZ
THE PHONE GOES DEAD
EVER DIALLED A WRONG NUMBER...?

ANTHONY
HOROWITZ
SCARED
IF YOU GO DOWN TO THE WOODS TODAY...

ANTHONY
HOROWITZ
KILLER CAMERA
IDLE HANDS DO THE DEVIL'S WORK...

ANTHONY
HOROWITZ
BURNT
HELL HATH NO FURY...

ANTHONY
HOROWITZ
THE NIGHT BUS
IT'S THE JOURNEY FROM HELL...

**Six spooky collections of short stories by Anthony Horowitz,
a master-storyteller and the best-selling author of the Alex Rider series**

Also available
as an ebook

www.orchardbooks.co.uk

ORCHARD BOOKS